KT-561-431

CASS AND THE **BUBBLE STREET** GANG

Scavenger Hunt

Erika McGann

illustrated by Vince Reid

THE O'BRIEN PRESS
DUBLIN

First published 2019 by
The O'Brien Press Ltd,
12 Terenure Road East, Rathgar,
Dublin 6, D06 HD27 Ireland.
Tel: +353 1 4923333; Fax: +353 1 4922777
E-mail: books@obrien.ie.
Website: www.obrien.ie
The O'Brien Press is a member of Publishing Ireland

ISBN: 978-1-78849-093-1

Copyright for text © Erika McGann 2019
Copyright for typesetting, layout, editing, design and illustration
© The O'Brien Press Ltd

All rights reserved.
No part of this publication may be reproduced
or utilised in any form or by any means,
electronic or mechanical, including photocopying,
recording or in any information storage
and retrieval system, without permission
in writing from the publisher.

1 3 5 7 8 6 4 2
19 21 22 20

Cover and internal illustrations by Vince Reid.

Printed and bound by Norhaven Paperback A/S, Denmark.
The paper in this book is produced using pulp from managed forests.

Published in

DUBLIN
UNESCO
City of Literature

X074506

Scavenger
Hunt

PHOTO: JOE BUTLER

ERIKA MCGANN lives in Dublin in her own secret club-house (which is actually an apartment) and spends her time solving mysteries and having brilliant adventures (well, she writes about them anyway). She likes cold weather (because it's an excuse to drink hot chocolate by the gallon) and cheesy jokes (because cheesy jokes are always funny, even when they're not funny). Her other books about Cass and the Bubble Street Gang, *The Clubhouse Mystery*, *Making Millions* and *Diary Detectives* are also published by The O'Brien Press. *Making Millions* was the UNESCO Dublin City of Literature 2018 Citywide Read for Children.

*For Sam, Damhan,
Séamus and Sadhbh*

Acknowledgements

As always, thanks to Vince Reid, Helen Carr, Emma Byrne and all at O'Brien Press. And to my niece, Amara, who loves Cass as much as I do.

Chapter One

Have you ever been so excited about something that your feet felt fizzy and you thought your tummy might explode? I have. I had that feeling when I was marching down the laneway beside Mr McCall's field; one hand was holding the printout of a flyer my parents got by email, and the other hand was pulling a shopping trolley full of detective brain-exercising equipment. I was on a mission.

In case you don't already know me, my name is Cass and I'm a genius detective. I solve mysteries, fight crime and

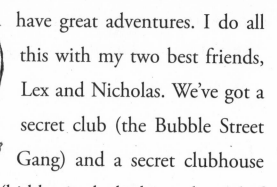

have great adventures. I do all this with my two best friends, Lex and Nicholas. We've got a secret club (the Bubble Street Gang) and a secret clubhouse (hidden in the hedge at the end of Mr McCall's field), and I'm only telling you this on the understanding that you tell NOBODY ELSE. This is top secret, highly classified, zip-your-lip kind of information. Understood? Good. Then I'll get on with the story.

When I got to the clubhouse Lex and Nicholas were already there. I slammed the flyer down on the clubhouse table, making Lex jump (she was in the middle of eating a mini Victoria sponge and she gave herself a strawberry jam moustache).

Nicholas turned the flyer so he could read it.

PUMPKIN FESTIVAL
ROWAN TREE MANOR

Celebrating autumn through the arts,

food & drink, and family activities!

Featuring:

Botanical Gin Distilling Experience

Bramble Patch Pumpkin Picking

Literary Explorations through the Bespoke

Walled Gardens

Fairy Trail Adventure

Scarecrow Scavenger Hunt

and much more …

Click <u>here to download festival brochure</u>

'I heard about that,' said Nicholas. 'There's an art competition, and a couple of exhibitions I'm going to check out.'

Trust Nicholas to focus on the wrong thing entirely. I suppose he can't help it; he's really into acting and making costumes and all that artistic stuff. It comes in very handy sometimes.

I stabbed my finger into the important line on the flyer.

'That!' I said. '*That* is the bit we're interested in. The Scarecrow Scavenger Hunt. A *scavenger hunt*. And we are going to win!'

Definition of scavenger hunt: an epic battle of wits and talent and speed. A mind-boggling, puzzle-solving adventure, where only the best and the bravest and the smartest succeed.

'Where's Rowan Tree Manor?' asked Lex.

'It's Mr McCall's mansion,' I said. 'My mum said he started calling it that last year.'

'You mean we'd have to go into his garden?' Lex shuddered. 'But I heard he's got a mini jail for kids who sneak onto his land.'

'That's totally untrue.' I had no idea if it was true or not. 'But even if it *is* true, he's letting people in for the festival so he won't be locking anybody in a mini jail.'

'I dunno, Cass.' Nicholas was frowning. 'I think the scavenger hunt's for teens as well. If it's all about solving puzzles and stuff, how are we going to beat secondary school kids?'

I was so glad he asked. 'Practice!'

I pulled the shopping trolley over to the table and started unloading.

'What are these?' said Lex.

'Detective brain-exercising equipment.'

'It just looks like books.'

'Exactly! Books full of crossword puzzles.' I dumped a pile right in front of her. 'You get started on those. And Nick, you start on these.'

'It's Nicholas,' Nicholas snapped. 'And these aren't crossword puzzles.'

'No, yours are murder mystery novels. Start reading – I expect you to solve the murders before you're halfway through each.'

'Cass, I'm not reading all of these! They're way too long.'

'And I'm no good at crossword puzzles,' Lex said, looking worried.

I took a deep breath for patience. 'You have to practise your problem-solving skills – it's like exercise for your minds. Your brains need to be working at optimum capacity if we're going to beat all the other teams in the hunt.'

'Then where's your giant pile of books?' said Nicholas.

'I don't need books,' I replied, 'my brain is always working at optimum capacity. I need a different kind of training.'

'What kind of training?'

'We have to rebuild the obstacle course.'

'Awwrgh!'

Nicholas and Lex made the sound at the same time, and it made me suspicious.

A while ago we built an awesome obstacle course in Lex's back garden, so we could train to become a Super Sleuth Security Squad. I was excellent at giving the others orders during training (I'd promoted myself to general), but it didn't last long because the obstacle course got wrecked. Lex said she found dog paw prints in the garden, and Nicholas said some of the stuff had been chewed up, but I didn't see any of that and lately I'd been wondering if the sabotage really was dog-related.

'What's wrong with rebuilding the obstacle course?' I said, narrowing my eyes.

'Nothing,' Nicholas said quickly.

'I just …' said Lex. 'I mean … all the stuff is gone. And … and I don't think my parents liked it being in the garden.'

I narrowed my eyes even more (I could barely see out of them now).

'Why not?'

'Because …' Lex went on. 'I was on it all the time … like all day every day. And it got in the way of the washing line.'

That did make sense. Lex loves anything to do with running and jumping and climbing and hanging. It probably was hard to have all that temptation in her back garden. And I could see her getting in the way of her parents trying to hang out the washing.

'Actually,' I said, brightening up, 'maybe I don't need the full obstacle course. I just need to practise running faster for the scavenger hunt, right? The house graveyard would be perfect for that.'

'Why the house graveyard?' said Nicholas

'Cos there's some obstacles in the way – all those concrete squares and the starts of houses that never got built – so I can practise running fast without bumping into things, like in a real scavenger hunt. Plus, it's right outside the clubhouse so I can keep an eye on you two doing your problem-solving in here.'

'Oh goody.'

I frowned at Nicholas, but I was too excited to be mad.

'This is going to be the best mission we've ever had!'

Operation Scavenger Hunt

Chapter Two

After getting the best news in the world (that there was going to be a scavenger hunt), I then got the worst news in the world.

On Monday Mr Freebs told us that we were going to be helping out with a garden project outside of school. (That wasn't the worst news – I love when we leave school during school, like when you go on your school tour. It feels like you're on holidays).

The garden project was in Shady Oaks Nursing Home, a fifteen-minute walk from school. (That wasn't the worst news either. My dad works at Shady Oaks and I go there a lot. I really like it there).

We were being put into groups or pairs for the project. Lex was in a group with Arnie (who is really funny. I'd like to be friends with Arnie, but I splatted him in the face with blue paint once – while investigating the possible existence of an invisible boy – and now I don't think we'll ever be friends). Nicholas was paired with Eva (Eva is obsessed with movies and is constantly quoting from them, but that doesn't bother Nicholas so much because he's into movies a bit too). And me? I was being paired up with Nathan Wall. *Nathan Wall.*

That was the worst news in the world. Because Nathan is my archenemy.

Definition of archenemy: the absolute worst of the worst of all your enemies (enemy = bad, archenemy = WORST).

Even though I can't stand Nathan Wall, I can never get away from him because Mr Freebs (who is mostly very nice and fun) makes me sit beside him in class. Mr Freebs wants everyone to *get along*. He has noticed that Nathan and I do not *get along*. He makes us sit together hoping that we'll eventually *get along*. It has been many, many weeks now and we still do not *get along*.

And that's because Nathan is a snob.

'Have you seen the new *Star Wars* movie yet?' he asked as we walked to Shady Oaks.

It sounded like he was being normal and friendly. I was surprised.

'No,' I said. 'I didn't think it was out yet.'

'It's not,' said Nathan. 'Not until the weekend. I saw it at a special screening for VIPs. My mum's got a really important job, so she's a VIP. She knows everybody who's anybody, so we get to do stuff like that – see the big new movies before anyone else. It's deadly. What does your mum do again?'

'She's an Assistant Staff Officer in ...' I knew my mum's job title, but I couldn't remember the name of the thing she worked for. I guessed. 'The Hospital Agency.'

'Assistant? That doesn't sound very important. Bet you don't get any cool stuff cos your mum's an assistant.'

'I don't care about cool stuff.'

'Want to know what happens at the end of the movie?' Nathan grinned.

'No.'

'I'll tell you anyway. See, there's this–'

'Shut up!' I said, sticking my fingers in my ears.

Nathan kept grinning as he talked, and I could kind of still hear him.

'Blaah, blaah, blaah!' I sang to drown him out. 'Blaah, blaah, blaah, bla-bla-bla-bla-bla-bla-blaaaaaaaaah!'

I could tell it was annoying him, so I sang the last *blah* really loudly and stuck out my tongue and everything.

'Cass, what on earth are you doing?!' Mr Freebs must have shouted because I heard him over myself. 'That's no way to behave in the street. You're very lucky to get this trip outside of school, and I expect you to behave exactly as you would in my classroom. Is that clear?'

'Yes, Mr Freebs,' I said to the ground,

feeling everyone stare at me.

I knew Nathan wasn't staring at me. But I knew he was smiling.

I hate Nathan Wall!

The garden project should have been fun. Shady Oaks has a really big garden and there's lots of different parts to it. There's a pond in one bit, lots of flowers in another, then there are sections with trees and benches and a new fountain.

Lex's group were planning a fairy village for their section, with tiny fairy houses hidden in the bushes and up the trees. It would be a really cool surprise for grandkids of residents who came to visit. I would have loved to work on the fairy village.

Nicholas and Eva were planning a 'red'

plot. They were going to use lots of plants with the colour red in them – red flowers, red leaves, red vines. It sounded really dramatic. I would have loved to work on the red garden.

But I couldn't. Because I was stuck with Nathan.

'I don't like flowers,' he said. 'Flowers are lame.'

'You're in a garden,' I snapped. 'There are going to be flowers.'

'Not in my plot.'

'It's *our* plot.'

'Well, well,' Mr Freebs showed up, smiling at us, 'how are you two getting along?'

'Not very well,' I said, trying to sound polite. 'Nathan doesn't want any gardeny things in our garden.'

'I don't like plants,' Nathan grumbled.

'Oh,' said Mr Freebs. 'Well, have you got a garden at home?'

'Yeah.'

'And you don't like it?'

'I do.'

'Oh. What's in your own garden that you like, then?'

'Rocks,' Nathan said.

'Is that all?' said Mr Freebs.

'And gravel. Expensive gravel. It looks like gemstones.'

'Huh. And no grass or plants or anything?'

'There's grass, but the gardener keeps it really short. My dad won't have plants or flowers in the garden. He says they're too needy.'

'*You're* too needy,' I muttered.

'Now, now,' said Mr Freebs, 'I'm sure we can reach a compromise.'

The compromise ended up being mostly what Nathan wanted – a rock garden with lots of gravel and just a few measly plants thrown in.

'I'm thirsty, Mr Freebs,' I said, dying to get away from Nathan for just a few minutes. 'Can I go inside and get a glass of water?'

'Hmm,' said Mr Freebs. 'We haven't got the run of the whole place now, we're just visiting.'

'Oh, it's okay, my dad works here. I come here all the time, I know all the staff.'

'Well, then I guess it's alright. But be quick – you and Nathan still have lots to do on your … em, rocky plot.'

It was a like a breath of fresh air getting away from the garden. I was hoping to talk to my dad inside the centre, but I couldn't find him anywhere. So when I was passing the sitting room and saw Carmella, I went in and sat down.

I love Carmella. She's one of the residents at Shady Oaks. She has big, bright orange hair that makes her look a bit like a tree that's caught fire. She's always got lots of jewellery on, with blue and red and green stones, and bright red lipstick.

'Hi, Carmella, it's me, Cass.'

'Hello, deary, hello!'

Carmella always calls me 'deary' because she can't remember my name, even when I've just said it, but I don't mind.

'I'm just on a break,' I said, 'so I can't stay

long. My class are helping out in the garden.'

'What class is that, deary?'

'My class at school. Fourth class.'

'Fourth class? Oh, you must know Freddie. She's your age.' Carmella tapped her nose. 'And she's a divil.'

Freddie is Carmella's daughter, Frederica. She's grown up now, but sometimes Carmella forgets and thinks she's still a kid. I wish she was. Freddie did the funniest, wackiest things when she was a kid. Sometimes I think Carmella's brain tells her Freddie is still ten so that she can talk about all those funny things.

'Why is she a divil? What did she do?'

'Deary,' Carmella put her hand on my arm and went all serious, 'she crawled into a hole in the wall behind the chest of drawers, after the hamster went in there.'

'How did she get out?'

'She didn't. She got stuck. We had to call the Fire Brigade.'

'No way! Did they get her out?'

'Yes, but only after an hour. She went in further, looking for the hamster, then decided it was great fun knocking on the walls and scaring us all.'

I laughed out loud. 'Brilliant!'

'When they finally got her out, she was missing a shoe. I asked her where it went and she said the hamster ate it.'

'Did he?'

'Not at all. She'd seen a new pair she wanted and this was her chance to get rid of the old ones. Divil. Always the divil.'

'She sounds great.'

'Want to see a picture?' asked Carmella.

'Sure.'

She showed me the photo she'd shown me a hundred times before. It was in a big, gold locket around her neck, and Freddie looked about eighteen in it.

'Well,' I said, getting up, 'I'd better get back to the garden. Have a lovely day, Carmella.'

'Bye bye, deary.'

Back in the garden Mr Freebs was kneeling next to Nathan with a crate full of different plants, and Nathan was pouting.

'None of them. I told you, I don't like green. Just gravel is better.'

I sighed. It was going to be a long day.

Chapter Three

'Cass and the Diabolical Detectives,' I said, thinking aloud. 'No, Cass and the Intrepid Investigators. Wait, Cass and the Devious Daredevils. Ooh! Or what about Cass's Turbo Team?'

Nicholas's lip was curling. 'Nothing with "Cass and the" in it. It's *our* team name, remember.'

'Yeah, I know that. Hmm, how about The Okara Adventurers?'

'No.'

'Okey-d'Okara?'

'Nothing with your second name in it either.'

'Fine, fine. How about ...' I thought hard. 'The Original Crazy Amazing Reckless Adventurers?'

Lex nodded. 'That's fine with me.'

Nicholas squinted his eyes for a second. 'Do the first letters make up your second name?'

'No,' said Lex. 'O-C-A-R-A.'

'I thought we could spell crazy with a "k",' I said, 'to be different.'

'No!' said Nicholas. 'Knock it off, Cass, we're not just *your* team.'

'Okay, okay. How about we all suggest names, and if you don't like a name you can veto it. We all get one veto each.'

'Yeah, let's do that.'

'Cool!' said Lex. 'How about … Puzzle Pals?'

'Veto,' I said.

'Oh.'

'Sorry, Lex, but it has to be something that'll intimidate the other scavenger hunt teams. Puzzle Pals is way too nice.'

Definition of intimidate: to scare the pants off everyone by being way better than them at everything.

'How about,' said Nicholas, 'Rosencrantz and Guildenstern and Yorick's Skull. That sounds pretty scary.'

'What?' I said. 'That's ridiculous. What does that even mean?'

'They're characters from Shakespeare.'

'No way. Veto.'

'You already used your veto.'

'Well I'm using it again.'

'You can't,' said Nicholas. 'You can only use it once.'

'Then I'm using it for that one.'

'So we can go with Puzzle Pals?' asked Lex.

'Urgh,' I said, shaking my head. 'No way. Veto.'

'You just used your veto for the Rosie Bildenstern Skull one.'

'Yeah, because I *had* to.'

'So Puzzle Pals is still in.'

I tried a different approach. 'I haven't suggested anything yet. How about The Terrible Tenacious Trio?'

'Veto,' said Nicholas.

'Why?'

'Cos it's terrible.'

Lex clapped her hands. 'So it's Puzzle Pals!'

'Veto!' I said.

'You haven't got any vetoes left, Cass,' said Nicholas.

'Do *you* want to be Puzzle Pals?'

Nicholas shifted his feet and looked away from Lex.

'No, but ...'

'Look,' I said, 'why don't we leave the team name for a while. It's just making us all annoyed.'

'You're the only one who's annoyed.'

'Cos you're the one who's being *annoying*, Nicholas.'

'Stop, please,' Lex cut in. 'I don't want to fight about it. I don't mind what name we have.'

'Let's just decide later,' said Nicholas, frowning at me. 'We have until Saturday to register.'

'Fine with me,' I said.

In my head I was already making a new list. If we were going to intimidate the other teams then we needed a name that would scare the *pants* off them.

I was back in hell (otherwise known as the garden at Shady Oaks).

Mr Freebs finally found a kind of plant that Nathan didn't hate. They're called *succulents*; they normally live in the desert and they have thick, spiky leaves (like a cactus) and you hardly ever have to water them. The only bad thing about them is they don't like the cold, so we had to plant them in pots that could be taken indoors in wintertime.

'They're not like proper plants,' Nathan said, very happy with himself. 'They look like they're made of plastic, and they don't have flowers.'

I'd snuck in a couple of succulent plants that *would* grow flowers, but I didn't tell Nathan that. I also didn't tell him that I was sick of hearing about all the famous people his mum knew. When he started listing them again, I said, 'I'm actually gonna have a walk around and check out the other plots. You know, see if there are any cool rocks left that we can add to ours.'

I am probably the most patient and peaceful person I know.

Lex's fairy village looked brilliant. There

were all these teeny, tiny houses tucked into the bushes, but you had to go looking for them. It was like a tiny treasure hunt. I even found a miniature playground that made me feel bad about my sad little rock garden.

Nicholas's red garden wasn't looking very red yet, but some of the plants had reddy-coloured leaves, and Mr Freebs showed us pictures of what the other plants would look like when they had flowers. It was going to be epic.

I wandered around to the fountain and found Mr Fox working at a picnic table. Mr Fox is one of the Shady Oaks residents – I don't know him very well, but I know he's into arty stuff. Any time I see him he's painting or drawing or making things out of paper.

He was making a big collage at the picnic

table; a picture made by gluing lots of pictures on top of a piece of card.

'Hi, Mr Fox,' I said. 'What are you making?'

Mr Fox looked up at me, not smiling.

'Catherine, is it?'

'Cass.'

'Hmm. I'm making a yellow rose.'

There was no way he was making a yellow rose. There were some yellow pieces of magazine, but loads of them were gold and brown and even black. He wasn't being very friendly, so I didn't ask any more questions, but since he didn't tell me to leave either, I kept watching.

It was weird. The more I watched, the more the picture did become a yellow rose. Kind of.

In the top left-hand corner the picture started out as black, then became brown and bronze and gold, and then finally, in the bottom right-hand corner, it was bright yellow. Even though the pictures were of cars and trees and buildings and things, from far away Mr Fox had made them look like the shape of a rose.

'That's brilliant,' I said.

'You still here?' said Mr Fox.

'Yeah. Your picture's brilliant. What are

you putting on it now?'

'More glue. It'll need to dry for a while and then I'll varnish it. Don't touch it now.'

'I won't. Can you teach me how to do that?'

'Teach yourself, it's not difficult.'

'Okay.'

I made a mental note to ask Mr Freebs if we could make collages next time we did art class. I'd ask my dad to look up a tutorial online before it, and then I'd make the best one. Maybe even better than Mr Fox's yellow rose.

Finally, the day of the scavenger hunt arrived.

Mr McCall's gardens were way bigger than I'd thought. The garden right behind the house (that backed onto the horsey field where our clubhouse was) was just one of the gardens. There were much bigger ones to the side of the house, with statues and walls and trees. There was a pond and a great big greenhouse full of exotic looking plants; there was even a hedge maze – though if I stood on my tippy toes I could just about see over it, so it wasn't a very tall one.

'There's a pumpkin patch out through that archway,' Nicholas said. 'I heard some other kids talking about it. There are loads of scarecrows in there – it sounds really creepy.'

The pumpkin patch *was* really creepy. There were about a dozen scarecrows, all with different costumes and faces. Some were messy, with straw poking out of their shirts and under their caps, and some were really neat with old-fashioned dresses and suits with top hats. Big black crows, who didn't seem at all scared of the scarecrows, picked their way through the pumpkin patch, staring people down and taking off into the air with shiny, black wings.

'This is so freaky,' said Nicholas.

Suddenly I jumped and grabbed hold of his arm.

'Oh my god, I forgot!' I said. 'I forgot to tell Mum to register us for the scavenger hunt online. How did I forget?!'

During the week I'd been so distracted with practising running, and making sure Lex and Nicholas did their brain-exercising, that it had totally slipped my mind.

'It's alright,' said Lex, 'my dad did it. He was buying tickets for my parents and your parents for the gin-making thing, so he told your mum he'd register us for the scavenger hunt too.'

I heaved a sigh of relief. 'Lex, your dad is the best! Seriously. Thanks so much.'

'No problem.' Lex was smiling, but it was kind of a weird smile. 'We'd better go round to the starting point.'

'Wait,' I said as she backed away from me. 'What name did you pick? Lex, what team name did you pick?'

'Em,' Lex called as she jogged away, 'I couldn't remember what we decided on, so I just …'

'What? What name?'

'Puzzle Pals.'

'No. Lex, *noooooo*!'

Chapter Four

We stood in the front garden of Rowan Tree Manor with all the other teams. I was still cringing at our terrible team name.

Puzzle Pals. Ugh!

Most of the teams were made up of primary school kids, but there were two teams of teenagers. The oldest team didn't seem to be taking it seriously – I think they were a bit embarrassed that all the other players were younger kids. Two of them wore old-looking t-shirts with the names of bands on them, and the third one had an earring in the top of his ear, and a nose ring as well (he had a cold because he was sniffing a lot, and I wondered if he was avoiding blowing his nose cos he was afraid the ring would get caught in his hanky). They made lots of noise teasing other teams and yelling out jokey rhymes like they were the clues, but they weren't. After a while they were already looking bored and I figured they'd drop out of the game early on. The oldest team weren't a threat.

The second teen team had Bianca on it (Bianca lives on my street, and she thinks she's the bee's knees. She's definitely not a genius detective, like me, but she is pretty fast). It also had Arnie's older brother on it. Arnie was playing too, but on a different team (which included Carol from school and two other kids I didn't know). Arnie is funny, but he's not very brainy and he's not that fast.

I decided Bianca's team were our main problem.

And also the Na-Sa-Ji Club. I hated to admit it, but they were a threat.

The Na-Sa-Ji Club are a (not very secret) secret club. They're made up of Nathan and his two best friends, Sasha Noonan and Jim Brick (Na-Sa-Ji comes from first two letters of each of their names – *so* unimaginative). Me, Lex and Nicholas accidentally found out about their secret club when we were investigating who had been invading our clubhouse (it was actually Lex's granny and her poker-loving mates, but that's old news now). In trying to find out who had been invading *our* clubhouse, we accidentally dug up the Na-Sa-Ji Club's club-*box* (which was full of

secret Na-Sa-Ji Club stuff). We reburied the box and never let on that we found it. Even though I don't like them, I still feel a bit weird and guilty for invading their privacy.

Nathan is definitely not a genius, but he's an okay runner. Sasha's fast and pretty smart – she gets the same grades as Nicholas at school – and I had a feeling Jim might be a bit of a dark horse when it came to solving riddles. He doesn't get great marks at school, but he has street smarts.

Definition of a dark horse: someone who is good at something, but nobody knows they're good at it until they do the thing in front of everyone, and then everyone's surprised. Not sure where it came from – maybe there was a horse who was good at something unusual, like knitting or something, but it didn't want people to know so it hid in a cupboard. But then one day someone opened the cupboard door and it was all dark inside, and then they saw the horse knitting and they were like, 'Oh, it's dark, horse. And you're good at knitting? I never knew!' and it became a thing.

Mr McCall stood in the porch of the mansion. I don't think I'd ever seen him that close before. He had a round face with rosy cheeks, and he wore a v-neck jumper over a polo shirt. He looked like he was about to play golf. And he didn't look happy that his garden was filled with loud kids scraping the gravel and flattening the grass.

'Can I have everyone's attention, please!' a voice called above the crowd. A thin man with blonde hair was walking through the groups, handing out envelopes. 'My name is Graham, and I want to welcome you all to Rowan Tree Manor's first ever Scarecrow Scavenger Hunt!'

There was lots of cheering and clapping.

Graham is Mr McCall's boyfriend (and *way* friendlier than Mr McCall – nobody would have cheered for *him*). He used to live on the other side of the country where he was in charge of an arts festival or something. When he moved to our town he had to give up his job, and that's when he set up the Pumpkin Festival at Rowan Tree Manor – probably so he wouldn't get bored.

'I'm giving each team a sealed envelope,' Graham said loudly as he walked through the crowd. '*Do not* open it until I say so.

Inside are the scavenger hunt clues. Now you all got the rules when you registered, but just to recap; you can solve the clues in any order you like; you'll need to take a photo of each answer – only *one* photo per answer, no hedging your bets by taking pics of every single thing you see.' There was some giggling from the crowd – I bet that's what a few teams had been planning to do. Graham went on. 'You need to submit the photos via the app as you go. When you've solved all the clues, and submitted all your photos, you need to get back to the starting point and click FINISH. The team with the most correct answers wins. If two or more teams have the same score, then the team with the fastest time wins. That all clear?'

'Yeah!' a few people yelled.

'I didn't hear everyone there.' Graham put his hand to his ear. 'I said, *is that all clear*?'

'Yeah!' everyone chimed in this time, giggling.

'Are you ready?'

'Yeah!'

'Set!'

There was scuffling as people got ready to open their envelopes and run. I squeezed my mum's phone in my hand while Nicholas tucked his thumb under the seal of the envelope.

'*SspplzzZZZZZZZZzzzzz.*'

We all jumped as Graham made a loud duck noise with a plastic whistle-thing, then we giggled, then we all got serious and ripped open the clues to the scavenger hunt.

Nicholas held the sheet of paper out for me

and Lex to read. I tried to speed read down the clues, but my heart was beating so hard it made me dizzy. I blinked a few times and reread the first clue:

> *Find me standing, tall and proud*
> *Fit to burst, but never loud*
> *I wear a glass so I can see*
> *The feathered beasts that I make flee*

I was trying to think, but some teams were already running and it made my head go scatty.

'Feathered beasts,' Nicholas was saying. 'Beasts with feathers – that's got to be birds, right? Like the crows. It makes them *flee*, like run away … It's got to be one of the scare-crows, right? Cass? *Cass!*'

'It's one of the scarecrows,' I said, my brain suddenly kicking into action. 'Come on!'

Lex took the phone as we ran around the house and through the archway to the pump-kin patch. There were already several teams in there, picking through the pumpkins and arguing with each other. I could see Alanna Mitchell from our street – she had Dev Bahl on her team (which made sense, cos he's fast), but also her little brother, Barry (he is not fast – bet her dad made her include him).

'It's a scarecrow,' she was hissing at Barry. 'Just take a picture and let's go!'

She's wrong, I thought, *it's not any old scare-crow.*

Find me standing, tall and proud. Some of the scarecrows were taller than others.

Fit to burst, but never loud. Some of them

had bellies stuffed full of straw, and some were skinnier.

I wear a glass so I can see.

'Wear a glass so I can see…' I mumbled.

'Hmm?' said Lex.

'Not glass*es*,' I said, still thinking, '*glass*. Like just one. What's that called, Nicholas? The thing they used to wear in olden days, with top hats and stuff.'

'A monocle?'

Trust Nicholas to know something so random.

I glanced quickly around the patch, spying the scarecrows with fancy, old-fashioned costumes.

'There!' I said, spotting a top hat. I ran to face the scarecrow and cried out, 'There! He's got a monocle!'

Lex ran up to me and took a photo of the scarecrow.

'That one!' Alanna pointed in my direction. 'Don't send the photo yet, it's *that* one!'

'Urggh,' Nicholas growled as every team in the pumpkin patch ran towards us. 'We're gonna have to be more stealthy if we want to win. No more giving the answers away, Cass.'

'Sorry.'

I meant it. That was a rookie mistake. One I wouldn't make twice.

Chapter Five

> *I could lie and say I'm cold,*
> *Empty, dark and full of mould*
> *But there is no point, you see*
> *Everyone can see through me*

Me, Lex and Nicholas were hunkered down on the far edge of the hedge maze. We couldn't afford to give any more answers away.

'I could lie and say I'm cold,' I read from the clue list. 'So, if they're lying that means they're not cold. They're warm.'

'Then they're also lying about being empty and dark and full of mould,' said Nicholas. 'So that means they're … full and light. And not mouldy.'

'I don't get it,' said Lex.

I didn't either.

'Skip to the next bit,' Nicholas said. 'There's no point in them lying, cos everyone can see through them. Hmm.'

'See *through* them,' I said. 'They're see-through! Like a window. You can see through a window.'

Nicholas looked up at the house. 'There's a million windows around here. Which one?'

I tuned out the other two as I thought about it.

Warm, lots of light, glass …

'It's the greenhouse!' I cried.

'*Shh*,' said Lex.

'Oh yeah, sorry.' I lowered my voice. 'It's made of glass so all the light gets in, it's hot inside and it's full of plants!'

'Brilliant, Cass.' Nicholas was smiling.

We ran around the hedge maze, past the pumpkin patch and down the rock garden to the big greenhouse.

As Lex took the photo and sent it through the app, I saw movement in the bushes at the top of the garden. Alanna peeked her head over the leaves and pointed at us.

'No!' I said. 'We're being followed.'

'They're going to steal all our answers,' said Nicholas.

'That's cheating!' cried Lex.

'Don't worry,' I said. 'I've got an idea.'

Four legs good, two legs bad
Don't get close or make me mad
A girl with long socks carries me

'It's a dog!' I cried, loud enough for the sneaky team to hear.

'That was quick,' said Nicholas. 'Are you sure?'

'Four legs good, two legs bad. It's got four legs and you don't want to make it mad. It's one of Mr McCall's growly dogs.' I faked looking around. 'But where does he keep them?'

Nicholas realised what I was doing and gave me an exaggerated frown. 'I've no idea. Maybe the kennels are down by the big trees.'

Out of the corner of my eye I saw Alanna whisper something urgently to Dev. Then he smiled and the whole team took off.

They knew where Mr McCall's kennels

were (so did I – they were on the opposite side of the house), but a dog wasn't the answer.

'Pippi,' I said, smiling.

'Huh?' said Nicholas.

'Pippi is the clue.'

'Your little sister, Pippi?' said Lex, looking very confused. 'How would she know where the dogs are? She's only two.'

'My mum named Pippi after Pippi Long-stocking,' I explained, 'from the books.'

'A girl with long socks,' said Nicholas.

'Exactly! Pippi Longstocking had two pets – a horse and a monkey.'

Nicholas nodded. 'And she was really strong and carried the horse around.'

'So the answer's a horse!'

'But you said the answer was a dog,' said

Lex.

'Keep up, Lex,' I said. 'That was to get Alanna's team off our tails.'

'So, where's the horse?' asked Nicholas.

I thought there must be one in the gardens – a statue or something – but I couldn't see one anywhere.

'Maybe it's in the house,' I said, not sure of myself. 'In a painting or a photo or something.'

Nicholas shook his head. 'That seems like a long shot. We could be searching the house for hours – it's massive.'

He was right. I closed my eyes and recited the rhyme to myself over and over.

'Don't get close or make me mad,' I said, opening my eyes. 'Maybe that's exactly what they mean. Don't get close to the *real* horse.'

'The one in the field!' cried Nicholas. 'How did we forget that?'

Scrabbling through the big conifer trees at the end of the garden, we pushed our way to the fence. Swishing its tail in the middle of the field was the horse. From a distance, Lex took a photo.

'Brilliant,' she said.

The rules of the scavenger hunt meant we could solve the clues in any order we wanted – we had been doing them in the order on the list, but lots of teams were doing that and it made it easier for them to follow us. I decided to change it up and go for the second last one instead.

But that clue had me stumped.

> *Atop of all That live below*
> *i'm full of Things they can't let go*
> *with rumours there's a ghost In me*
> *i wish the world Could let me be*

'Someone's really bad at typing,' I said, as we stood by the pond. 'All those small *i*'s where there should be big ones. Mr Freebs would scribble all over that with his red pen.'

'Never mind that,' said Nicholas. 'What's the answer?'

'Hmm.' I thought really hard. 'I don't know.'

'What are we up to?' a voice whispered on the other side of the hedge.

'This is number four,' said another one. 'Come on, come on, it's down here.'

That was Bianca's voice. And there was

her team; racing out from behind the hedge maze and heading towards the greenhouse.

'They've got four,' Nicholas said. 'They're ahead of us. We need to get this one, Cass. Think, *think*.'

'I'm trying,' I said, racking my brains. 'Atop of all That live below. It's something high up.'

I looked around. The conifer trees were really tall, but I couldn't see anything at the top of them except leaves. Since the answer was 'full of Things', it couldn't be leaves. A couple of the stone statues were tall – and maybe one of them 'had a ghost' in it – but none of them could be 'full of Things' either. There was a crow-shaped weather vane on top of the shed, an old-fashioned lamp hanging from the top of a tall pole and a birdhouse

stuck high up on the back wall of the house, but none of these sounded right. *What was it?*

'The attic!' Lex said suddenly.

'What?'

'A-T-T-I-C.' Lex pointed to the clue. 'All the capital letters in the clue spell ATTIC.'

I was so excited I grabbed the sleeve of her jumper and shook it.

'Lex, you're a genius!'

She grinned.

'Come on,' Nicholas said, grabbing the two of us and running. 'We've gotta get ahead of Bianca's team.'

Arnie's team were in front of us as we reached the front door of the mansion. When they went in we heard a sudden shout along with screaming and giggling.

'I think something's about to jump out at us,' I said. 'Brace yourselves.'

We all slowed down as we walked through the door, waiting for a fright. But nothing came.

The hall was huge, with a pale floor that

looked like marble, and a great big sweeping staircase. There were paintings on the walls with fancy gold frames, lots of ornaments, more statues (but these were smaller than the garden ones and made of bronze) and a sparkly chandelier hung over it all.

Arnie's team had run up the stairs – we could hear them on the first floor – but otherwise the hall was empty.

'Come on,' I said, 'we've gotta get a photo of the attic.'

'*BEWARE!*'

Something orange leapt from behind the bannister and shrieked with its arms wide. I jumped back off the first step and screamed. And then giggled.

It was a scarecrow with hair made of chunky orange wool wearing a worn, plaid jacket. Bits of straw stuck out from his cuffs and around his collar. His face was painted white with bright red circles for cheeks, but I could recognise Graham's friendly grin underneath it.

'Beware the ghost in the attic,' he said, still waving his arms.

We giggled again and slipped past him to climb the stairs, Lex holding on tight to my arm.

'Beware!' Graham wailed behind us. 'Beware the ghost of Rowan Tree Manor!'

We climbed the next flight of stairs to the second floor. Beneath us we heard more screaming and laughing.

'Bet that's Bianca's team,' said Nicholas. 'We'd better get a move on.'

It took a few minutes to find the stairs to

the third floor, and even longer to find the entrance to the attic. We wandered through hallways covered in paintings and mirrors. There were landscapes and fields of flowers, pictures of stormy seas and eerie old paintings of people staring out from the walls.

'There it is!' said Lex.

There was a creaky set of wooden stairs tucked into one corner at the end of the hallway.

Nicholas nudged me in the back.

'You first.'

I stood on the first step and looked up into the dark, musty-smelling attic. It was quiet up there. But that didn't mean it was empty.

Chapter Six

The steps were the kind with gaps underneath them, so when I got near the top I put my hands on the top step to make sure I could get into the attic safely. I was afraid if a ghost jumped out at me I'd lose my footing and fall down the stairs.

But I doubted anything would pop out. Graham was the scarecrow on the ground floor; I couldn't see Mr McCall joining in to be the ghost in the attic.

'Come on up,' I said, standing. 'There's no-one up here.'

Lex and Nicholas followed me.

There was one small window in the slanting

roof, but otherwise the attic was dark. There was stuff everywhere – metal trunks stacked on the floor and lots of things wrapped in cloth leaning against the walls.

'Let's get the photo and get out of here,' said Nicholas.

Lex held the phone up, but her hand was shaking.

'Do you think there's really a ghost?'

'No,' I said, but I had no idea.

If there was a ghost in the mansion, this was definitely the spot it would pick to hang out.

'Em …' Lex was still holding up the phone, but she couldn't keep it still long enough to take the photo.

'Here,' I said, taking the mobile. 'I'll do it.'

I waited for the image to clear, making sure

to get the window so it would be obvious it was the attic, when something moved in the corner of the screen.

I frowned. There was a sheet hanging off an old chest of drawers on one side of the room, but it was moving. By itself.

I gulped. 'What is that?'

'What's what?' said Nicholas.

The sheet fluttered. Lex and Nicholas noticed this time.

'What *is* that?' Lex gripped my arm.

A weird voice whispered across the attic. '*The ghooooooooost.*'

The sheet billowed, getting bigger and bigger, until suddenly it sprang from behind the chest of drawers and screeched.

I screamed and dropped the phone. Lex nearly toppled out the door of the attic –

Nicholas caught her just in time. Seconds later the sheet and two other people were laughing their heads off.

'*Nathan*!' I yelled. 'I'll get you for that!'

Sasha pulled the sheet off her head while Nathan and Jim nearly collapsed on the floor laughing.

'That wasn't funny,' Nicholas snapped.

'It was for us!' Nathan said, wiping a tear from his eye. 'Aw, just realised – we should've recorded it.'

'Way ahead of you,' said Jim, holding up the phone in his hand.

The three Na-Sa-Jis burst out laughing again while me, Lex and Nicholas scowled.

'Yeah, really original,' I said, trying to hide that my hands were still shaking. 'Sheet over your head for a ghost. Like that's never been

done before.'

'Whatever, losers,' Nathan said, still giggling as the three of them pushed past us and headed down the steps. 'Enjoy losing the rest of the hunt, *losers*.'

I picked up my mum's phone, hoping it wasn't broken.

'Do you think they're going to show that video to people?' asked Lex. 'I nearly fell down the stairs.'

'That's why it wasn't funny,' said Nicholas.

'Who cares if they do,' I said, pretending I didn't. 'Who wouldn't get a fright if something jumped out at them in a dark attic?'

Nicholas sighed. 'They're probably ahead of us in the scavenger hunt too.'

'No way,' I said, holding up the phone and finally getting a photo of the attic. 'But we still have to hurry. We've got lots of other teams to beat.'

Find the spot in Rowan Tree
Where you can always see the sea
But only in the northern view
Is the beacon in the blue

This one had everybody stumped. We could tell because there were a bunch of teams running in and out of rooms on the second and third floors of the mansion. Most of the doors were locked, but there were a few open on each floor.

'This one. No! This one.' Arnie was leading his team down the hall. 'Actually, do you know what? It should be on this side.'

Carol was rolling her eyes. 'Oh my god,

Arnie, just pick a door!'

Bella and Jack from our street came bar-relling past them with Bella's little cousin. I think they were the youngest team playing, and they were so excited they kept getting the giggles. They nearly ran us over as we climbed the stairs.

On the third floor I stood on a tiny balcony in one room, straining my neck trying to see the sea in the distance.

'Is that it?'

I pointed to a blurry blue line between the land and the sky.

'That's cloud,' said Nicholas. 'I think it's raining over there.'

'Isn't that weird?' Lex said. 'That it's rain-ing over there and we can see it, but it's not raining over here. Weird.'

I blew a sigh out of my nose like an angry bull.

'We're not high enough. We need to be higher.'

'There is no higher,' said Nicholas.

I smiled. 'Of course there is! The attic.'

Lex's face fell. 'I don't want to go up there again.'

'I know,' I said, trying to be sympathetic. 'But you have to. I need all of us.'

Up in the attic I kneeled down on the floor, like a table. Nicholas stood on my back and gave Lex a leg up.

The window was high, but we'd done this before to get over the high wall of the empty house (the empty house is at the end of our street. We used to call it the empty house because nobody lived there and we thought it was haunted. Our friend, Martyn, moved in with his family though, so now it's not haunted or empty).

My arms were shaking as Nicholas balanced on my back, holding Lex up as high as he could.

'Can you see anything?' I said, grunting with the effort. 'Can you see out the window?'

'Yeah,' Lex replied. 'Ooh! I can see Alanna and Dev in the garden. Aw, I think Barry's annoyed – he's sitting on the edge of the pond and he won't move.'

'Never mind about that. Do you see the sea?'

'Em … no. It looks like it did downstairs, but with more clouds. Maybe if it's not cloudy at all you can see the sea from here.'

'No,' I said. 'The clue says you can *always see the sea* from this spot. It doesn't say you can see the sea *if* it's a really clear day and you're standing on two of your friends.'

'Well,' said Lex, 'then maybe this isn't the spot.'

'Okay. Get off me.'

With Lex and Nicholas off my back, I got to my feet and brushed the dust off my jeans.

'You can always see the sea,' I muttered to myself. '*Always* see the sea.'

'It doesn't make sense,' Nicholas said. 'It's got to be the attic window – it's the highest point in the house. If you're going to see the sea from anywhere, it's here.'

'Urrgh,' I growled, with my face in my hands. 'That's not right. But I don't know what else it could be.'

'We have to send a photo of something, and a guess is better than nothing. Lex, take a pic of the window and send it.'

'No!' I said. 'It's not right.'

'Then what is it?' said Nicholas.

He sighed when I didn't reply.

'Fine,' I said. 'Send a photo of the window.'

It was killing me as Lex took the photo. She lowered the phone and was about to click, SEND.

'Wait!' I said, holding my hands out.

'Cass,' said Nicholas, 'we have to move on. We're wasting time.'

'It's not the attic window,' I said. '*Always* see the sea. I know where you can always see the sea!'

'Where?'

I grinned, turned and raced down the stairs.

Chapter Seven

'Oh,' Nicholas said as we stood in the hall-way.

In front of him was a painting of a cliff overlooking the sea.

Lex tilted her head and squinted.

'That was a bit of a confusing clue then,' she said. 'It didn't say *picture* anywhere in it.'

'It didn't have to,' I said, smiling. 'Turn around.'

On the opposite wall was another picture of the sea, but this one was stormy. The waves were crashing over a lighthouse.

'Now turn to your left,' I said.

The painting straight ahead, at the end of

the hall, was one of the sea at nighttime.

'And now this way.'

Opposite the nighttime painting, far away at the other end of the hall by the attic stairs, was a painting of a boat on the ocean.

'See?' I said, turning Lex around and around. 'No matter which way you turn, from this spot you can *always* see the sea.'

'Oh. Okay.'

'Can't believe you got that, Cass,' said Nicholas. 'You really are a genius.'

I grinned. 'I know.'

'So which picture do we take a picture of?'

I read the second half of the clue.

'But only in the northern view, Is the beacon in the blue.'

'How do we know which way is north?' asked Lex.

I grinned again, jammed my hand into my pocket and pulled out a compass.

'How did you know to bring that?' said Nicholas.

'Cos in books,' I said, 'all the best scavenger hunters carry a compass. It's essential equipment.'

I held the compass still and waited for the needle to settle. It pointed right at me. I

turned around to see the stormy sea painting.

'The lighthouse!' I said. 'The lighthouse is the beacon in the blue.'

'Brilliant,' said Nicholas.

Lex took the photo just as Bianca appeared in a doorway halfway down the hall with the rest of her team right behind her (they must still have been trying to see the real sea from a balcony). Lex's arms snapped to her sides, but I saw Bianca smile. She'd seen us take a photo of the toughest answer in the scavenger hunt.

'Let's go,' I said. 'We've gotta get all our pics in before they do.'

The last few clues were no challenge for me. It was just a race against time now.

One was really short:

> *I've got the tools, but ask me why*
> *Unlike my friends, I'll never fly*

'It's the crow weather vane,' I said. 'Got wings but it can't fly. It's on top of the shed outside. We'll get that one when we're back in the garden. Finish the indoor ones first.'

Looking very impressed, Nicholas read out the next clue.

> *'I get short as I grow old–'*

'Mr Manning!' yelled Lex.

'What?'

'Mr Manning next door …' Lex was blushing. 'He's kind of old, and I think he's getting shorter …'

'It's a candle,' I said. 'A candle gets shorter as it burns down. I've heard that riddle before.'

Nicholas went on.

'*And my home is made of gold, I'm not alone, I've friends you see, We share a branch, but there's no tree.*'

I thought for about a second and a half.

'It's one of those fancy branchy candle-sticks with lots of candles in it. A gold one.' I narrowed my eyes and thought back. 'There was one on the table in the hall when we came in. Near the front door.'

'Cass, you're starting to scare me,' said Nicholas.

'I know,' I said, being serious. 'I'm that

good.'

We were back outside for the next clue because I'd also worked that one out.

> When it's windy I get wrinkles
> I get bigger when it sprinkles
> From the platform, facing southwest
> Take a picture of my house guest

'How did you know?' Lex asked as we ran around the house and across the garden to the pond.

'The water gets ripply when it's windy,' I said, puffing as I ran, 'like wrinkles. And when it rains it gets bigger, cos it's filling up with more water.'

'Getting kind of sick of calling you brilliant,' said Nicholas.

'Well don't,' I said. 'You'll be calling me that for rest of our lives.'

We arrived at the pond out of breath. Across the garden, the Na-Sa-Ji Club were also running.

'Did you only get that one now?' Nathan yelled. 'We got the pond ages ago.'

'We're not doing them in the same order, *Nathan*,' I yelled back, but he was already gone.

'Quick,' said Nicholas, 'which side?'

There were two slabs of stone on either side of the pond. I took out my trusty compass and hopped onto one.

'That way's north,' I said, pointing and working it out in my head. 'So that means southwest is … it's the other one, quick!'

Lex leapt onto the other slab and went to

take a photo.

'Wait!' said Nicholas. 'We've to take a picture of its house guest. Who's the house guest?'

I looked into the pond. In the murky green I saw something big and orange moving around.

'There!' I said. 'It's a giant goldfish.'

'Koi,' said Nicholas. 'It's called a koi fish.'

I rolled my eyes. 'Really? Do we care right now? Take the picture, Lex.'

Nicholas grinned. 'Just the weather vane left.'

I'd never run so fast. I ran so fast I even kept up with Lex.

The last clue. We were on the *last* clue. We were going to win!

I was running so hard I felt kind of sick.

When we got to the shed I felt even sicker.

'Where is it?' said Nicholas. 'You said the weather vane was on top of the shed.'

'It was,' I said. 'I saw it.'

'Then where is it?'

We searched high and low. There was nothing on top of the shed. There was nothing on the grass in front of the shed. There was no weather vane *inside* the shed. The shed backed onto an overgrown field full of real crows that flew overhead and squawked at us. We searched the long grass of the field in case someone had thrown the weather vane from the roof. The crows kept squawking. It felt like they were tormenting me.

We didn't find the weather vane.

Bianca's team won the scavenger hunt. I

explained to Graham about the weather vane.

'Gosh, that's only new!' he said. 'It's just gone? I am sorry. Don't know what could have happened to it.'

He apologised again and said he was leaving that photo out of the judging – we didn't need the weather vane photo to win. But Bianca's team still won because they had finished quicker.

'Because we spent *ages* looking for the weather vane at the end!' I cried to my mum on the way home. 'I *knew* the answer to the clue so we didn't want to give up and go back to the start without having all the photos. If we'd gotten the weather vane photo at the beginning of the hunt we would've finished before Bianca's team, I *know* it. *And* she got the answer to the hardest clue from *us*. She cheated. We didn't cheat at all, and we were the best team in the whole thing and we still lost!'

'I'm sorry, pet,' my mum said. 'I really am. But it's not the end of the world.'

It *was* the end of the world. At least that's how it felt.

Operation Scavenger Hunt
FAILED

Chapter Eight

At school the next day I had to sit next to Nathan, as usual. He grinned when I sat down.

'You didn't win the scavenger hunt yesterday.'

'You didn't win either.'

'Yeah, but we weren't trying to win, we were just doing it for the laugh.'

I screwed my face up. 'You *so* wanted to win. I saw the three of you running across the garden like there were monsters after you. You were trying so hard to win.'

'Nah, we were just having a laugh,' Nathan sneered. 'You lot were serious though. You actually thought you'd win – bet you bawled your eyes out on the way home.'

'I did not.' I didn't actually cry on the way home, but I could have. I was that upset.

'You were whining to Graham about the weather vane, I *heard* you.' Nathan started making this high-pitched whiny voice. '*That's not fair, there was no weather vane. We should've won, wah-wah-wah.*'

My blood began to boil, and then it hit me like a concrete block.

'*You* stole the weather vane,' I said.

'What?'

'You stole the weather vane – that's where you were running to when we were at the pond; the shed. You stole the weather vane so we couldn't win.'

Nathan rolled his eyes. 'Oh my god, you're

such a loser. Who would bother stealing a weather vane? You probably stole it so you could whine about not winning.'

My face was pinched up so tight it was nearly hurting. 'You made us lose the scavenger hunt. You did it on purpose. I *know* you did.'

Nathan laughed. 'You should see your face – you take this stuff so seriously. You're such a loser.'

I stared at him with his smug grin and his greasy smug hair and his smug *Star Wars* pencil case signed by George Lucas, and something inside me snapped. I shoved his pencil case off the table so all his stuff went flying.

'Cass Okara!' Suddenly Mr Freebs was standing right in front of me. 'What has gotten into you?'

I didn't know what to say. I stared at the floor.

'You're going to pick up Nathan's things,' Mr Freebs said, 'apologise, and then you are going to tidy the classroom while everyone else is outside for break. Is that clear?'

'Yes, Mr Freebs,' I mumbled.

'And?'

'Sorry, Nathan.'

The words stuck in my throat. I slid off my chair and picked up all of Nathan's pens – some of them had rolled halfway across the floor. Lex gave me a sympathetic look when I picked up the biro under her chair.

After school I sat in the clubhouse fuming.

'What did you want to call it?' asked

Nicholas.

'Operation Catch the Cheating Cheaty Cheaters,' I said, folding my arms.

'That's catchy.'

'Well, what do you wanna call it then?'

Nicholas sighed. 'I don't know, maybe nothing. Do we really need an operation for this, Cass? I'm gutted that we lost as well, but is it really that big a deal?'

'Not a big deal?' I said, my voice getting louder. 'They *cheated*.'

'But why?' said Lex. 'They didn't win either.'

'To make us *lose*. And maybe they thought they could win if we lost.'

Nicholas didn't look convinced. 'We don't even know if they got a photo of the weather vane. Maybe they didn't. Maybe it was gone by the time they got to the shed – it looked like they were heading that way when we were at the pond.'

'*Exactly*,' I said. 'That's when they stole it.'

'I don't know,' said Lex, avoiding my gaze. 'I don't think any of them had a bag or anything. If they stole it, where did they put it?'

'They *hid* it,' I cried, 'obviously.'

'I don't know.'

I couldn't believe the two of them. Why didn't they care? I felt so mad at both of them.

'When you needed money for your art class, Nicholas, we did Operation Make Loads of Money for you.' Tears were starting to well up in my eyes, but I forced them back down. I didn't want to cry when I was trying to make a point. 'And Lex, when your granny was breaking into our clubhouse we didn't get mad – we built her her own one.'

'I know.' Lex's voice had gone really quiet. 'That was really nice.'

'Then why won't you bother helping when it's something that's important to *me*?'

'We do,' Nicholas said, getting angry too. 'We do all the time. Just cos we don't want to look like whingers doesn't mean we don't care.'

'*Whingers*?!'

'Cass, you spent ages giving out to Graham after we lost, it was really embarrassing. Just let it go. Everyone will think we're just whining cos we lost.'

It felt like the tears were going to explode out of my face.

'Then *don't bother*!' I shouted. '*You're* the

whiner. You're always whining cos you're so selfish. I *hate* you!'

I stormed out of the clubhouse, slamming the door so hard behind me that I heard the walls shake.

The tears were streaming down my face as I marched down the laneway. I wiped them away before I got to my house.

I was in a really bad mood when we sat down to dinner. Dad had made akara, which is my second favourite dinner after lasagne (as long as he doesn't make them too spicy), but I was too upset to like them.

'They're too hot,' I grumbled, pushing the fried bean balls around my plate. 'You put too many chillis in them.'

'I only put a couple of chillis in the whole

batter, Cass,' Dad replied, 'and I left out most of the seeds.'

'They're still too hot.'

My dad turned back to his dinner and sighed loudly out of his nose, which is what he does when he's done arguing with me. Mum tried instead.

'Just eat some bread with them, pet. Do you want some mayonnaise?'

'I don't like mayonnaise!'

I do like mayonnaise. Mum knows that, so she stopped arguing with me as well.

After sitting there for a while with my arms folded, I got annoyed that no-one was getting mad that I wasn't eating my dinner.

'They're too hot! I don't like them when they're too hot!'

'Cass, that's enough,' my mum said. 'Go to

your room.'

I stood up and stomped out of the kitchen. Then I stomped up the stairs, into my bedroom and slammed the door.

I flopped onto my bed feeling very sorry for myself. Mr Freebs was mad me. Lex and Nicholas were mad at me. Now my parents were mad at me. I bet Pippi and Ade, the annoying baby twins, would have been mad at me too if they hadn't been too busy throwing their dinner at each other (my parents *never* give out to them for that – two-year-olds get away with anything).

I was so angry and upset it was like there was a balloon swelling up in my chest and I didn't know how to let it out.

A little while later my mum came up to my room. Even though I was being kind of bold, she was nice to me. Somehow that made the balloon get bigger and bigger until finally it burst and I bawled my eyes out.

'I know you're upset about the scavenger hunt, sweetheart,' my mum said, wrapping me in a big hug.

'Lex and Nicholas are mad at me,' I said, sniffing. 'And Mr Freebs gave out to me at school.'

My mum hugged me tighter. 'I'm sure Mr Freebs won't be mad tomorrow,' she said. 'And Lex and Nicholas won't stay mad either. This will all blow over soon, pet, I promise. I bet you a plate of your dad's akara that you'll feel much better in the morning.'

She gave me a sneaky look when she said that, and I gave her one back.

'No way – there's too many chillis in them.'

'Cheeky,' my mum said, and she tickled me until I squealed and rolled off the bed.

Chapter Nine

My mum was right.

In the morning I got up, washed my face, narrowed my eyes and gave myself a good glare in the mirror.

This was not how a genius detective handled things – yelling at her friends and giving out to everyone. I was still angry, but I was going to put that anger to good use.

'Hey, Cass.' Lex looked at me as if I was going to pounce like a lion when I saw her at school. 'I'm really sorry about yesterday.'

'No, *I'm* sorry,' I said. 'I shouldn't have yelled at you. Can we still be friends?'

'Of course!'

'Oh, good.' Nicholas had appeared behind me. 'I was afraid that fight would go on for ages.'

'I'm sorry, Nicholas,' I said firmly, so he'd know I was serious. 'I shouldn't have shouted–'

'Never mind that, I'm sorry too. Are we going to investigate the weather vane thing or what?'

'Seriously?' I said.

'Yeah,' said Nicholas. 'You were right. This is important to you, and that means we have to help. Clubhouse Rule number ten.'

I smiled. It felt so much better *not* fighting with my friends.

'No way, no more plants! I just want rocks.'

It was a gorgeous day in the Shady Oaks

garden. The sun was shining and the birds were singing. Unfortunately I was stuck gardening with Nathan Wall, so it felt more like a miserable, rainy afternoon when you're bored and have nothing to do.

'You've only let me put in *two* plants,' I said.

'And that's enough.'

'What about that big gap?' I said, pointing. 'It just looks empty. What are you going to put in there?'

'More gravel.'

I sat back on my heels, took a deep breath and counted to ten in my head.

'I'm thirsty,' I said finally. 'I'm going inside for a glass of water.'

I found my dad in the big sitting room. Carmella was in one of the armchairs and he was kneeling next to her, holding her hand. She looked like she'd been crying.

'Dad?' I said quietly, stepping into the room.

'I don't have time to talk today, honey,' my dad said. 'Carmella's upset.'

'What happened?'

'My locket,' Carmella said between sobs, grasping at her blouse where her locket should have been. 'My Freddie.'

'The gold one?' I asked.

'It's gone missing,' said my dad. 'I don't think I've ever seen her take it off, but she didn't have it this morning. Can't find it anywhere.'

Two carers, Mary and Lucinda, were

looking under the furniture and going through all the stuff on the shelves.

'I don't get it,' said Mary. 'It's just vanished.'

'They stole it,' said Carmella.

'Who?' I said. 'Who stole it?'

Carmella didn't answer. I don't think she knew.

She'd been crying so hard her eyes looked swollen. She looked like I'd felt the night before. I knew how horrible that was.

I thought of all the times Carmella had shown me the picture of Freddie in her locket – how she never remembered that she'd shown it to me before. Maybe she'd forget she'd lost it. And then she'd notice it was gone and she'd get upset all over again. That would be terrible.

I knew what I had to do.

'Don't worry, Carmella,' I said. 'I'll find your locket.'

The Bubble Street Gang already had one operation on the go, but we were never too busy to squeeze in another one.

Operation Stolen Locket

That Saturday Dad was working, and he let me, Lex and Nicholas tag along.

'We're going to search for Carmella's locket,' I told him. 'You'll find it quicker with more help.'

I didn't mention that we were also planning to question the staff and residents of Shady Oaks (and possibly interrogate the more suspicious ones – that means questioning them, but without mercy).

'We'll have to split up,' I whispered to Lex and Nicholas in the car, 'and question people separately. There's too many of them otherwise.'

'On our own?' said Lex.

'Yes.'

'But I'm not good at talking to people.'

I couldn't argue with that, but we had no choice.

'I'll give you a list of the nicest people there, Lex. Me and Nicholas will tackle the tougher ones.'

'Oh. Okay.'

She still looked worried.

It was another sunny day and, when we arrived, loads of residents were walking in the gardens.

'Eh, we'll stay out here for a bit, Dad,' I

said. 'Make sure Carmella didn't drop her locket in the garden.'

'Good idea, honey. See you inside.'

I waited until Dad had disappeared through the doors, then turned to Lex and Nicholas.

'Alright, Operation Stolen Locket is on. Remember, you can be polite, but don't pull your punches.'

'I'm not punching anybody!' said Lex.

'Not literally,' said Nicholas. 'She means don't go too easy on them.'

'That's right,' I said, gazing across the garden full of innocent-looking older people. 'Somewhere out there is a ruthless locket thief. Everybody ready?' Lex didn't look ready, but there was no time to waste. 'Get to work!'

My questioning of possible witnesses and/ or suspects went very well. Edwina Barnes was sticking out as the most obvious culprit.

She smiled a lot and talked about her grandson's brilliant exam results (note: her grandson's exam results were not that impressive), but what made alarm bells ring in my head was the amount of jewellery she wore.

'This?' she said, turning in her wheelchair so she could show me the bracelet up close. 'I got this for my birthday … hmm, ten or twelve years ago now. Isn't it lovely? And the ring? You've a good eye.' She winked. 'Won't tell you how much, but this one's worth a pretty penny.'

'You like jewellery then?' I said, writing it all down in my Top Secret notebook.

'Ooh, I love it,' she replied. 'But most of

it isn't expensive – just this ring. I'm always losing things, you see, but my daughter gets me more. I'm like a magpie – I'll go for anything shiny!'

'Is that right? Thanks very much for your time, Ms Barnes.'

I knew exactly what had happened. Edwina Barnes had spotted the gold locket around Carmella's neck and swooped in like an evil bird. It was an open and shut case.

'It was George Murray,' Nicholas said when the Bubble Street Gang met up at the fountain. 'George Murray stole the locket.'

'It was Edwina Barnes,' I said, frowning. 'I'm sure of it.'

'Did Edwina Barnes have a feud with Carmella that started over a favourite table in the dining room and has been going on for years?'

*Definition of feud: a fancy word for a big,
long fight (I'm pretty sure). Definitely the sort
of word Nicholas would use.*

'No,' I said, 'Edwina Barnes is not having a
feud with Carmella – as far as I know – but
she will go for anything shiny. She said so
herself.'

'It was George Murray.'

'Lex,' I said, getting impatient, 'who've you
got?'

'Em ...'

Lex looked down at her notepad. I noticed
there were very few notes on it.

'Did you question anybody?' Nicholas
asked.

'Yes.'

'Did you *interrogate* anybody?' I asked.

'Em … I did learn a lot about Mr Kane's dogs. They were all terriers, and he used to do all the dog shows–'

'Urgh, Lex! You were supposed to be ruthless in your questioning. Not talk about their hobbies!'

'I'm not good at being ruthless.'

I looked at Nicholas.

'We're going to have to question Lex's list again.'

'Don't bother,' said Nicholas. 'I'm telling you, it was George Murray.'

'I'm going inside,' I snapped. 'There are loads of residents we haven't even checked out yet.'

'Well, I'm staying out here.' Nicholas sat

down on the edge of the fountain. 'It's nice and sunny, and I've already found the thief.'

I marched past him in such a hurry I nearly knocked over Carmella. She was walking the path around the garden and had stopped to smell a bunch of yellow roses growing near the door.

'Hey, Carmella.'

'Hello, deary, hello!'

She looked much happier. I wondered if she'd forgotten about her locket. I decided not to remind her.

'Nice roses,' I said instead.

'Don't you just love the yellow ones?'

'Sure.'

I wasn't really listening. Edwina Barnes was making her way into the centre; a carer was pushing her chair from the garden to

the door. As they went through the doorway something small dropped to the floor.
A green bead from the fancy cardigan Ms
Barnes was wearing. I automatically moved
forward to go pick it up, but someone else
was much faster. A quick hand shot from
behind the doorframe and snatched the bead
from the carpet.

'Bye bye, deary,' Carmella said as I ran past
her.

'Oh, sorry, bye, Carmella.'

I saw him. But only his back as he went
through to the main hall. He wore a blue
jumper.

By the time I reached the main hall there
were a number of blue jumpers, pottering
between the sitting room, hall and dining
room.

I had a suspect. A *real* suspect. But which one of them was it?

Chapter Ten

'What was George Murray wearing?' I said, a little out of breath after running back into the garden. 'A blue jumper?'

'No,' said Nicholas, 'a brown jacket.'

'Then it wasn't George Murray.'

I told Lex and Nicholas about the bead-snatcher. They both agreed it was a good lead.

'Come on,' I said. 'We've got suspects to question. Any man in a blue jumper.'

It turned out blue jumpers were quite popular among the men in Shady Oaks.

'And where were you exactly half an hour ago?' I said, trying not to yawn as I questioned the millionth blue jumper (at least it felt like the millionth).

'Choir practice,' the blue jumper replied.

That was an alibi I could check out, and he didn't look worried.

Definition of alibi: when someone says you did something bad, but you totally couldn't have because you were at the cinema with your cousin or something, and you have the ticket to prove it.

'Thank you for your time,' I said, striking his name off in my notebook.

'That's it,' said Nicholas, 'that's all of them.'

'Then we've already questioned him,' I said, 'and he was too clever to give himself away. We need a new plan.'

'What kind of plan?' asked Lex.

'A set-a-trap-for-him kind of plan.'

'You mean like covering a hole in the ground with leaves and stuff so he'll fall in?' Lex said. 'That sounds mean. And what if he gets hurt?'

'Not a *booby* trap, Lex, we're not going to hurt anyone.'

'You mean set him up,' said Nicholas.

I smiled. 'Exactly.'

Lex's dad came to pick up Lex and Nicholas five minutes later (Nicholas had acting class, and Lex had running club), so I was left to set up the locket thief on my own.

I borrowed a shiny trinket from Carmella – she let me have a silver hair pin with sparkly stones in it – then I walked around the centre looking for blue jumpers. As soon

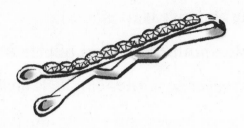

as I spotted one I'd make sure I was in his eye-line, then I'd accidentally (on purpose) drop the hairpin and walk away. I was so good at it, Nicholas would have been proud of me. I even spied on each suspect without giving myself away, by using a little hand mirror. I'd hold it in the palm of my hand, low down and hidden by my fingers, then I'd point it behind me as I walked away. I could see exactly what the blue jumper was doing. It was genius.

But not genius enough. None of the blue jumpers snatched the hairpin. Two of them did pick it up, but only to tap me on the shoulder and give it back.

The blue-jumpered locket thief was clever. But that was fine with me. I like a challenge.

The Bubble Street Gang hadn't forgotten about Operation Scavenger Hunt (updated name: Operation Catch the Cheating Cheaty Cheaters – not everyone had agreed to the updated name though. Nicholas suggested Operation Weather Vane instead, but I don't think it's as good). I was still convinced the Na-Sa-Ji Club were guilty of stealing the weather vane.

'But how can we prove it?' asked Nicholas. 'The weather vane is long gone, and none of them would ever admit it to us.'

It was a tough case.

'We should examine the crime scene,'

I said. 'There might be some evidence left behind.'

I was so hoping we'd find Nathan's *Star Wars* wallet, or Sasha's earring, or Jim's … I couldn't think what Jim might have dropped by the shed, but I was still hoping he'd dropped it.

In the driveway of Rowan Tree Manor the recycling bin had been left out. It was over-full.

'Look,' Nicholas said, lifting the lid a little. 'The weather vane *was* new.'

On top of the bin was a flattened box with a photo of the crow-shaped weather vane on the front.

'Forty centimetres wide,' I said, reading the dimensions on the side of the box. 'Difficult to hide that down your jumper without bits poking out.'

'I didn't notice Nathan looking pointy.'

I scowled and snapped the bin lid shut.

'We've only started investigating. Come on, let's go ask if we can check out the shed.'

We rang the bell and Graham answered the door with a big smile.

'Well if it isn't the Puzzle Pals! How're you three doing?'

I cringed at our awful team name (sorry, Lex), then got on with the mission.

'Hi, Graham,' I said. 'We were wondering if we could have a quick chat about the weather vane–'

'Oh, I am sorry about that. Shocking business really. Who'd steal a weather vane? It's not like it's worth much. Looks like it went missing early on in the game too – only two teams got a photo of it in the end.'

'Really?' asked Nicholas. 'Which two teams?'

'Hmm, now let me think.' Graham scratched his chin. 'There was the Spaghetti Yetis, and then ... that's right, The Time Lords. That was the winning team, wasn't it?'

'Yeah,' I said, with a twinge of pain in my chest. 'Time Lords won.'

I could feel Nicholas looking at me.

'Would you mind if we had a quick look at the shed?' I quickly asked Graham. 'We're pretty good at solving mysteries – we might be able to figure out where the weather vane got to.'

'Ooh, a band of investigators, are you? That sounds like fun. Knock yourselves out. It's dinner time for the dogs, so they're in their kennels – won't bother you.'

'That's great, thanks Graham.'

As we jogged around the house and through the gardens towards the shed, Nicholas was still looking at me. But it was Lex who said it.

'The Na-Sa-Jis didn't get a photo of the weather vane. So that means they didn't steal it.'

'They still could've stolen it,' I said, not wanting to let it go. 'Just to stop us winning.'

'Doesn't make sense,' said Nicholas. 'You know it doesn't. If they stole it, why not just take the photo first?'

I sighed. It didn't make sense.

'Let's just check out the crime scene first,' I said, 'before we make any final decisions.'

The crows in Rowan Tree Manor were not

your usual kind of crows. Firstly, they were not scared of scarecrows (during the scavenger hunt some of them were *sitting* on the scarecrows in the pumpkin patch), and secondly, they weren't at all scared of people either.

When we arrived at the shed there were crows on the roof, on the fence behind the shed, and on the ground. And not one of them moved. They turned to look at us, and they flitted around a bit when we got closer, but none of them flew off.

'Is it just me,' said Lex, 'or are crows kind of scary?'

These fearless ones with shiny, black feathers and shiny, black eyes were kind of scary. I liked them.

Me, Lex and Nicholas tiptoed around the

creepy crows – they watched us like they knew exactly what we were doing – searching for something of Nathan's or Sasha's or Jim's. We didn't find anything.

'We should take a look at the roof,' I decided, 'to see if there's any damage. Either one of them climbed up there, or they knocked the weather vane off by throwing something at it – rocks maybe.'

'I don't like the crows,' Lex said, knowing she'd be the one that would have to climb onto the roof.

'They're fine,' I said, clasping my hands to give her a leg up. 'They're nice, look … with their lovely black beady eyes. That don't blink.'

Lex was shaking a little as I boosted her up onto the shed roof.

'Any damage up there?' I called.

'Hang on.'

There was silence for a few seconds. As Lex inspected the roof, I watched a crow pick up a skinny bit of metal in its beak and poke it into a tiny hole in a log that ran along the bottom of the shed. It needled out a little insect, then dropped the little metal bar and ate it.

'Aren't you clever,' I whispered.

'No,' Lex's voice suddenly called out, 'no damage. There's the little stand thing with teeny hooks for the vane to fit into, but it's not dented or anything.'

'Have a look for anything they might have dropped up there,' I said, 'a button or a torn bit of a jumper … or a hair. *Anything.*'

'A hair?' Nicholas raised an eyebrow.

'I could examine it under my microscope,' I said.

'I can't see anything like that,' said Lex. 'Just a few leaves … and crows.'

'Face it,' said Nicholas, 'the Na-Sa-Jis didn't do it.'

He was right. But it hurt.

'Fine,' I said. 'But if it wasn't Nathan, then who?'

Nicholas reached up to grab Lex's feet as she slid down from the roof.

'It's not easy getting up there,' he said. 'And whoever did it had to be quick so they wouldn't be seen.'

'Okay,' I said.

'Bianca? Or one of her team?'

'They did win,' I said. 'And they are all taller than us.'

'Worth checking it out?' said Nicholas.

'Oh yeah,' I said, feeling better already. 'We're coming for you, Time Lords.'

Chapter Eleven

Back at Shady Oaks Lex's fairy village and Nicholas's red garden were both ahead of schedule (and I, of course, was trying to get away from Nathan again, if only for a few minutes), so we asked Mr Freebs if we could go visit some of the residents before our class finished up in the garden for the day. Mr Freebs said that was fine (because he didn't know we were also planning on doing a little investigating during the visit).

I'm normally extremely clever – that's why I'm a genius detective – but I had a minor brain blip that day.

Definition of brain blip: when your brain kind of hiccups and doesn't work properly for a second, and you do or say something stupid that you wouldn't normally do or say.

'If all three of us set the shiny trinket trap,' I said to Lex and Nicholas as we walked through the main hall, 'then there's a chance the locket thief will fall for one of them.'

'You mean try setting a trap for every single man in Shady Oaks?' said Nicholas. 'There's way too many of them, Cass, it would take hours.'

'Not for every one,' I tutted. 'Just the ones in blue jumpers.'

'That was Saturday. Do you not think he might have changed his clothes?'

Blip.

That was my brain blipping. *Of course* he would have changed his clothes. There was no telling what the blue-jumpered locket thief would be wearing now.

'Umm …' I mumbled.

Nicholas didn't say anything. He just gave me a look like he felt sorry for me because I was so dim.

'I'll come up with something else,' I snapped. 'You guys go look for anything suspicious while I have a think.'

'What do you mean, suspicious?' asked Lex.

'You know … *anything*.'

'Just wander around, looking for anything,' Nicholas said.

'Yes, *Nicholas*.'

He gave me another look as he and Lex

walked away. I was a bit embarrassed and annoyed, so when I got into the sitting room I kind of flopped into a chair and sighed out loud. How did I not think of the locket thief changing his clothes since the weekend?

'Are you alright?'

Edwina Barnes was sitting next to me.

'I'm fine, thanks,' I said, 'I've just been a bit stupid.'

'Well, I was just about to head to the dining room for a piece of cake. Would some cake cheer you up?'

'Thanks,' I said, 'but I'm okay. Plus, I don't have much time. I'll have to go back to school soon.'

'Alright, pet. Well, you have a nice day.'

I sighed again as Ms Barnes and her carer, Lucinda, left the room. They bumped into a nurse on the way out, and something clattered to the floor with a flash of silver. It was the nurse's badge – the flash was the silver clasp – and a hand shot out to grab it just as it hit the floor.

'Oh,' the short man said, realising what it was and handing it back, 'this is yours. I thought it was … never mind.'

Ms Barnes's. He thought it was some shiny trinket of Ms Barnes's that she wouldn't miss; something he could steal and get away with it.

There he was. *The locket thief.*

I ducked behind water coolers and dodged tea trolleys as I followed the short man down the hallway.

He turned right past the dining room, and

then left into one of the wings of residents' rooms. I had ducked behind the corner at the turn of the corridor, but popped out just in time to see the door of Room 25 close behind him.

I could have questioned him alone, but since I'd been an absolute genius and spotted the thief all by myself, I wanted Lex and Nicholas (especially Nicholas) to be there when I got the full confession.

'Are you sure about this?' Nicholas said as the three of us stood outside Room 25 a few minutes later.

'Positive,' I replied, and knocked firmly on the door.

'Hello. Can I help you?'

The man who answered couldn't have looked sweeter. He had a little bowl of dyed brown hair sitting on top of his head, and big grey eyes that made him look like he was permanently smiling. But I wasn't fooled.

'Yes,' I said. 'We're … carrying out an investigation on the premises, and we'd like to ask you a few questions.'

'Oh yes,' the man said. 'I remember you. Please come in.'

'That sounded very official,' Lex whispered to me as we went in.

I smiled.

'What's the investigation about again?' the man asked.

'We'll ask the questions, sir, thank you.' I put on a stern expression and consulted my notebook with all the blue-jumpered peo-ple's names. 'You are Mr Adrian Klein. Is that correct?'

'Yes.'

'And you have been a resident at Shady Oaks for two years, is that correct?'

'Yes.'

'Mmhmmmm.' I meant to carry out the official-sounding questioning a little longer, but I was too excited at having caught a real-life actual thief. 'And, Mr Klein, is it also correct that you have been stealing shiny trinkets from unsuspecting residents of Shady Oaks like some giant trinket-stealing magpie?'

Mr Klein blushed all the way to his bowl-shaped hair.

'Oh. Oh my.'

'That's right, Mr Klein, you've been caught red-handed! Now hand over Carmella's gold locket, and all the other stuff you've stolen, and we won't have to involve the authorities.'

'Carmella's locket?' he said. 'B-but I would never take Carmella's locket.'

'Mr Klein, I *saw* you. I saw you steal the green bead from Edwina Barnes's cardigan. We know you're the thief.'

'Well, yes.' Mr Klein blushed again and hurried to his chest of drawers. He gently lifted something from a dish sitting on top. 'Yes, I have been collecting Edwina's things. But … I'm going to return them all.'

In his hand was a loose chain of shiny trinkets. It was a mishmash of rings and beads and bracelets and pins, silver and gold, with blue and green and pink and red stones.

'You see,' Mr Klein went on, 'she doesn't realise she's lost them. So I've been looking for them, to make this beautiful necklace. It's a present for her birthday – a lovely necklace of all her lost things. Do you think she'll like it?'

It was the worst necklace I had ever seen. But I didn't say that.

'So you didn't take Carmella's locket?'

'No, of course not. I wouldn't do that – that's stealing.'

I believed him. I believed that he didn't take Carmella's locket. And I believed that he was making the worst-looking necklace in the world for a woman he liked.

Mr Klein wasn't the locket thief.

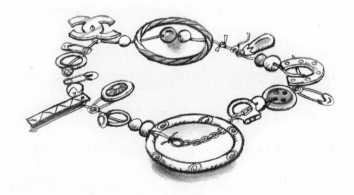

Chapter Twelve

Me, Lex and Nicholas were hunkered down behind a car opposite Bianca's house. We were on a stakeout. (The last time we did a stakeout, we made an amazing fake bin that all three of us squeezed into – but Bianca's house was a last-minute stakeout so we didn't have time to make a brilliant disguise. Besides, the amazing fake bin ended up being a magnet for yippy dogs and too small for us all to run in).

Bianca's friend, Tara – who had also been on the Time Lords team for the scavenger hunt – was hanging out at Bianca's house after school. At first they'd disappeared into the house, and we felt a bit silly hiding behind a car waiting for them to come back out, but now they were sitting on the wall of the front garden, checking their phones and chatting to each other.

Tara had a maroon mini-backpack on that she wore all the time. I remembered that she'd been wearing it the day of the scavenger hunt too.

'If that backpack's big enough to fit a weather vane,' I whispered, 'then the Time Lords had motive *and* opportunity.'

We weren't trying to listen in on their conversation, but being so close we couldn't help overhearing.

'And I was like, I don't *care* if you started wearing those bracelets first,' Tara was saying, 'cos like I've always liked them, and like I just wear them *more*. Like I've always had them.'

'Oh my god,' Bianca chimed in, 'I know. Like I started wearing them a *year* ago.'

'I never saw you wear them a year ago.'

'I totally always wore them. Like not *loads* of them together, but like I'd always have one on.'

Tara checked her phone again. 'Yeah, but loads of them is the thing. Like, we've *all* always had them, but Killian thinks he's the first one. Like he *always* thinks he invented everything.'

'Yeah, I know, like it's *so* annoying.'

Lex leaned on me to peek over the car bonnet.

'Do teenagers always talk like that?' she whispered. 'Are we going to end up talking like that when we go to secondary school?'

'I'd rather eat my own arm,' I replied.

'This is so boring my brain's going numb,' Nicholas said, readjusting his feet. 'And so are my legs.'

'We just need to get to that backpack,' I said. 'If it's wider than forty centimetres, then it was big enough to hide the weather vane.'

'How are you going to check?' said Nicholas. 'Are you planning to mug her in broad daylight?'

'No.'

'Then what?'

I reached into my pocket and pulled out a measuring tape.

'Are your pockets like Mary Poppins' bag?' said Nicholas. 'Can you just pull anything out of them?'

'It's not magic, Nicholas,' I said, looking down at him. 'I'm just prepared. Like any brilliant detective should be.'

'Well, brilliant detective, how are you planning to measure Tara's backpack without her or Bianca noticing?'

That was a good question.

'You two are going to have to distract them,' I said.

'How?' said Lex.

'You could have a fight. Yeah! A big shouty fight, and while they're watching I'll sneak up behind Tara and measure her backpack.'

'Fight about what?' said Lex.

'I don't know, anything. Just improvise.'

'I can't improvise. I'll say the wrong thing.'

'You can't say the wrong thing,' said Nicholas. 'That's what's so great about improvising.

You just go with the flow, say whatever you want – there are no wrong lines.'

'I can't.' Lex was already looking scared. 'I-I-I'll say something wrong. I can't make it look real.'

Nicholas sighed. 'What if Cass and I have the fight, and you measure Tara's bag?'

'Okay.'

'But what will we fight about?' I asked, suddenly feeling like I was on the spot. 'We need to decide.'

'No we don't,' said Nicholas. 'That's what's so great about improvising–'

'We have to agree on something to fight about, Nicholas, otherwise it won't look real.'

'It doesn't matter what you say, that's the point. Just go with it.'

'Oh really? Doesn't matter at all? So if I

said … I'm mad at you for wearing a frog as a hat, would that work? Can you improvise a fight about *that*, Nicholas?'

'They're coming this way!' Lex suddenly hissed.

'Nicholas, move!' I snapped as Bianca and Tara crossed the road towards the car. 'Crawl around to the back. Go, *go!*'

'My legs are dead!' Nicholas was trying to get out of sitting cross-legged without using his feet.

'Move!'

I pushed on Lex, who tried to lift Nicholas, who knocked her into me; I tipped back and sprawled over the curb, right in front of the car.

'Eh.' Bianca stood over me with a weird look on her face. 'What are you doing, Cass?'

Like a flash I zipped open a length of the measuring tape and pressed it to the road.

'Checking for sinkholes.'

'For what?'

'Sinkholes. You know, sinkholes can appear anywhere at anytime. They're these giant holes in the ground that just open up all of a sudden and swallow everything above them. I'm just, eh …' I pretended to carefully read the measuring tape. 'I'm just checking these cracks in the road. Checking they're not getting bigger.' I squinted up at Bianca and Tara. 'Just making sure there isn't a sinkhole on the way.'

Tara turned to Bianca. 'The kids on your street are weird.'

'You have no idea,' said Bianca.

They were walking away when suddenly

Nicholas popped up in front of them.

'Ow!' he yelled, suddenly grabbing his shin. 'Ow, my leg! I think it's broken.'

'What?' said Bianca. 'How did you break your leg?'

'Just there. Just now, when I fell. I think it's definitely broken. Can you call my dad?' He gestured to the phone in Tara's hand.

'Your house is right over there,' Bianca said.

'I can't walk that far. Can you please call my dad? *Please*? The number's O84 ... no, wait ... yeah, no, it's 084, then I think 93 ... no, wait ...'

While Bianca and Tara were distracted by Nicholas, I crept up behind Tara and held the measuring tape to her backpack. Twenty-nine centimetres. Not wide enough to fit the weather vane. Over Tara's shoulder I shook my head at Nicholas.

'Actually,' he said, standing straight, 'I think it's fine. Yeah, it's actually fine. Must have been a cramp or something. Thanks anyway.'

Tara frowned at Bianca as the two of them walked away. 'The kids on your street are *seriously* weird.'

'Good work,' I said to Nicholas, 'but her bag's not big enough.'

'If the Time Lords didn't take it,' said Lex, 'where did the weather vane go?'

I had no idea.

Chapter Thirteen

Our garden plots at Shady Oaks were nearly finished. I felt really bad about how long Operation Stolen Locket was taking, especially because I saw my dad comforting Carmella in the garden. She'd been crying.

'She noticed her locket was gone again,' my dad told me when I asked.

Poor Carmella. It must have been awful to forget and then remember it like it had just happened.

Inside the centre, I wandered around aimlessly looking for inspiration. How could I find the locket thief?

I wandered past Mr Fox's room, and the

yellow pictures on the walls were so inviting I knocked on the open door.

'Can I come in?' I asked.

'If you want.'

Mr Fox was sitting by the window, reading.

'I did a collage at school,' I told him. 'It wasn't as good as your yellow rose, but it was only my first go. I'll get better at it.'

'Good for you.'

Mr Fox didn't seem in the mood to chat, so I looked around at all his gorgeous pictures. He made every kind – collages, paintings, photographs, drawings – and loads of them had yellow roses in them. There was the bronze-brown collage, a painting of a really tall bunch of roses, and a single massive yellow rose in the middle of the wall – it had a gold centre, and curly sheets of yellow paper were the petals, so it was 3D.

Mr Fox even had a vase of real yellow roses on his chest of drawers.

'Lovely flowers,' I said. 'Where'd you get them?'

'The garden.'

'Hmm.'

He still wasn't in the mood to chat, but I didn't want to leave right away – the room was too lovely – so I stayed for a few more minutes until a magpie landed on the windowsill outside and made this loud chattery, squawk.

'Grr,' Mr Fox said, and rapped on the window. '*Magpies.*'

The bird flew off.

'I like magpies,' I said. 'They're really sure

of themselves – like crows.'

'They're too loud,' said Mr Fox, 'and there's too many of them.'

'Around here, you mean?' I said, suddenly interested. 'There are a lot of magpies around Shady Oaks?'

'Isn't that what I just said?'

I smiled.

'Thanks Mr Fox, you've been a great help.'

He gave me a crooked look. 'Whatever.'

I'd fallen through the giant winding worm tunnel, all the way through the earth, and down into Dungeon World. Don't feel sorry for me – I jumped in on purpose. My friend was missing, and I had to save her.

It was quiet in the Swamp of Lost Souls, but I'd have to keep my wits about me.

There were lots of icky creatures hiding in the muddy waters; sticky blue lizards, underwater weasels, fiery cockroaches ... not to mention the *Lost Souls*.

'Quick!' Lex ran at me from across the green. 'They're right behind me! *Run*.'

'What's right behind you?' I yelled, confused.

'The Lost Souls!'

'But wait,' I said as Lex flew past me, 'I haven't rescued you yet!'

I chased her over the green, nearly hitting Nicholas on the way.

'I thought you were stuck in the dungeons?' I said.

'You were taking too long to get to the dungeons, so I came to the swamp instead.'

He ran after Lex.

'Wait!'

I finally caught up with both of them at the end of the green, and I was really out of breath.

'Lex,' I gasped, 'I was supposed to rescue you.'

'I know, but it was taking ages and it was boring just sitting on the ground. I decided to escape instead.'

'But you didn't have the ring of power.'

'No, I just used a dagger to cut the ropes.'

I sighed. 'They were supposed to be *enchanted* ropes – a regular dagger shouldn't have worked on them.'

'I know, but I was *bored*.'

'If we're going to be in different parts of Dungeon World,' said Nicholas, 'then you need to move faster, Cass. Otherwise me and

Lex are wasting the game just sitting around.'

I didn't bother arguing (I was too out of breath to try anyway).

It was Saturday. The Bubble Street Gang were taking a break from our two operations (any decent detective will tell you that if you want to be good at work, then it is also *essential* to rest and play. We'd already rested by watching a movie in Lex's house, and now we were playing. Though I was so exhausted it kind of felt like work).

'I'm tired,' I said.

'Already?' said Lex. 'Want to play something else instead?'

'Anything where I don't have to run.'

We decided to head to the clubhouse. Halfway across the green we met Graham walking Mr McCall's dogs.

'If it isn't the investigators! How are you lot getting on?'

'Hey Graham,' I said, 'we're fine. We haven't figured out what happened to your weather vane yet, but we're still working on it.'

'Really? Well aren't you brilliant. I'd better fill you in on the latest development in the case then.'

'What's that?'

Graham took a quick look around, then whispered dramatically, 'They've struck again!'

'What?'

'Seriously. Bought a replacement weather vane – just put it up yesterday – and it's gone already.'

'No way!'

'I know,' he nodded. 'Shocking stuff. No

weather vane is safe apparently.'

'That changes everything!' I said.

'It does? Well,' Graham reined in the dogs that were getting a bit jumpy, 'I'll leave it to the professionals. If you find the culprit, you let me know.'

'We will.'

We waved as Graham walked on with the dogs.

'Does it?' asked Lex. 'Change everything, I mean.'

'Of course,' I said. 'It means it's got nothing to do with the scavenger hunt. It *never* had anything to do with the scavenger hunt. Someone wanted the weather vane itself. Bad enough to steal it.'

'But why?' said Nicholas. 'What's so special about a weather vane? And why steal two of them?'

'I don't know,' I said. 'But I'm going to find out.'

Chapter Fourteen

I was halfway up a very tall tree. It hadn't looked that tall when I started, but now that my arms were getting tired and there were still miles of branches above me, I realised it was a very tall tree.

Lex was already at the top of her tree.

'You okay, Cass?'

'Yep,' I said, grunting with the effort of the climb. 'I'm fine. Don't make me talk.'

'Okay, sorry. Nicholas, you okay?'

'Yeah, I'm grand.'

Nicholas was in the tree next to me, and that one seemed to have an inbuilt ladder; he was climbing almost as fast as Lex.

I finally reached the last big branch. It kind of curved out from the trunk, so I was able to sit into it, like a hammock, and have a rest.

'See anything in those nests, Lex?' I asked.

We were investigating magpie nests. There were a bunch of them in the trees, and I was sure one of them had Carmella's gold locket in it. Everybody knows that magpies steal shiny things – I've read it in loads of books.

'Hang on.' Lex grabbed a long twig and tiptoed out onto a branch like a tightrope walker.

'Don't touch the nests,' I said. 'And if there are any eggs or chicks in them, don't touch them either.'

'I know,' Lex said, peering over a fork of twigs to see into one nest. 'Nothing shiny in there. Just twigs and brown-looking stuff.'

'Next one then,' I said, still resting on the hammock branch.

It was Sunday and my dad wasn't working that day, but I pestered him so much about knowing exactly where Carmella's locket was that he eventually agreed to drive the three of us to Shady Oaks. While we stayed in the garden, Dad had gone inside for a cup of tea – I was glad because I hadn't mentioned that we'd be climbing the old trees in the corner and I'm not sure he would have been happy about it.

'Cass, look!'

Nicholas was pointing towards the fountain.

Edwina Barnes was sitting at a picnic table, and Mr Klein was handing her a package wrapped in colourful paper.

'Uh-oh,' I said, 'here it comes. The worst birthday present ever. She's going to hate it.'

'Do you think so?' said Nicholas.

'Unfortunately for Mr Klein, I do. Ms Barnes likes *fancy* jewellery – and that necklace is a disaster.'

'Poor Mr Klein,' Lex said, taking a break from the nests.

We watched as Ms Barnes unwrapped the gift. She paused for a second – *here it comes,* I thought – then her hands shot to her face and I could just hear,

'Oh my goodness!'

I was about to feel sorry for Mr Klein when Ms Barnes grabbed his arms and pulled him into a big bear hug. After she let go, she lifted the necklace to the light (and there was *loads* of necklace – there were giant brooches hanging off that thing), then put it over her head to hang around her neck.

'Huh,' I said.

Mr Klein pointed to the door and Ms Barnes nodded. He turned her wheelchair, and the two of them made their way into the centre.

'Must be going to lunch together,' said Nicholas. 'She must really *hate* that necklace.'

I rolled my eyes. 'I know you love it when I'm wrong, but I don't care this time cos that was sweet.'

'It was sweet,' said Lex.

'You looked in all your nests yet?'

'No. Have you looked in any?'

Lex doesn't usually get smart with me, so

I thought I'd better get to my feet and do some work.

Magpie nests are pretty impressive. From below they just look like a mess of twigs jammed into a fork in a branch, but when you get right next to them and look inside, the twigs are all flattened and smooth, like the inside of a cup. It does look like a comfy place to park your bum.

I didn't see any eggs in any of my nests – maybe it wasn't egg-time for magpies – but I did see a few weird-looking creepy crawlies on the trunk of the tree and the branches. Ugh.

I'd been very high up in the tree for a while, and my arms were even more tired from holding on for so long. I started feeling a little shaky too, so decided it was time to

get down.

'Did anyone find a locket?' I called out before I started the climb down.

'Nope,' said Nicholas.

'Not me,' said Lex.

'Me neither,' I said. 'I didn't find *anything* shiny in any of the nests. Maybe that thing about magpies stealing shiny things is not true at all – maybe the poor, innocent magpies are getting blamed for nothing.'

'Must be a human one then,' said Nicholas.

'Huh?'

'A human magpie. That stole the locket.'

'Oh. Yeah.'

We were back to square one.

'There's Carmella,' Lex said, pointing across the garden.

I felt bad. Carmella looked happy as she strolled along the path, but I knew that soon she'd look for her locket again and she wouldn't be.

She leaned over to smell the yellow roses near the door. I frowned.

'I've seen her do that before.'

'What?' asked Lex.

'Lean over to smell the roses.'

We watched as Carmella leaned so far down that her forehead touched the petals.

'You know, if she was wearing her locket right now,' said Nicholas, 'it would be hanging down, and could easily catch on something.'

'Like a thorn,' I said, 'or on a tangle of leaves or stems.'

'And then when she stood up straight–'

'The chain would snap, and bam!'

'Lost locket.' Nicholas smiled.

I forgot how tired I was as the three of us scuttled down from the trees and raced to the rose bush by the door. We got scratched by thorns and clung to by vines as we scoured the soil, but we didn't find anything.

'Oh well,' Nicholas said, 'it was a good idea.'

As Lex climbed out of the rose bush next to me, a yellow rose snapped back and hit me in the face. A light bulb lit up in my brain.

'Better than good,' I said. 'It was a brilliant idea!'

'But we didn't find the locket.'

'Yes we did. I know exactly where Carmella's locket is.'

Chapter Fifteen

'Good afternoon, Mr Fox.'

Mr Fox had the perfect name for a locket thief – because he was so *crafty*. Like a fox.

We were waiting outside his room after lunch when he came walking along the corridor.

'The one who likes magpies,' Mr Fox said drily as he opened his door.

'I do like magpies,' I said, 'but today … um, can we come in?'

'If you must.'

'But today,' I said, strolling into the room with Lex and Nicholas following behind, 'I'm after a different kind of magpie.'

'Is that right?'

'It is.' I waited for him to ask more, but he didn't. 'It's you, Mr Fox. You're the magpie.'

'Mm.'

He didn't sound at all interested. That annoyed me. I pointed a finger at the huge paper yellow rose on his wall.

'*That*,' I said, 'is Carmella's locket.'

He finally turned around and looked.

'That's a rose.'

'In the centre, the gold bit. That's Carmella's locket.' I walked closer. 'You know, when I first saw it I just presumed it was gold paint, but now I know better. That's actual gold.'

'It's a gold coin,' Mr Fox replied. 'I got it in a car boot sale.'

I looked closer at the golden circle that sat at the centre of those curling paper petals.

'It's got a tiny hinge on one side,' I said. 'It's a locket.'

'It's my locket.' Mr Fox wasn't ruffled at all. 'My sister gave it to me.'

I looked closer at the golden circle. There was the faintest hint of an engraving – nearly worn away – but it was there.

'There's a fancy 'C' engraved on the locket. It's Carmella's.'

'My first name is Clarence.'

'No, it's not,' I snapped, finally losing my patience. 'Your first name is … ugh, I can't remember, but it starts with an 'E' or something. It's definitely not Clarence anyway. I can check with my dad.'

At last, Mr Fox seemed to give in.

'Fine. I found the locket–'

'In the yellow rose bush, I know.'

He finally looked impressed at my detective skills.

'It was just sitting there in the soil, and I was missing a centre for my rose. It was perfect.'

'It was *Carmella's*.'

'I didn't know whose it was. Thought maybe a magpie dropped it.'

'So did we!' Lex said. 'Well, we'd thought maybe a magpie had stolen it. That's so funny that we thought the same thing.'

'Anyway Mr Fox,' I said, giving Lex a look, 'you know who it belongs to now. So give it back.'

Mr Fox took one last look at the paper rose, then he picked up a scalpel from his desk and carefully prised the golden locket out of its centre. The curly paper petals drooped, and he very gently pushed each of them back into place as if he didn't want to hurt them. When the locket was finally out, the rose looked kind of sad and empty, and I couldn't help feeling sorry for Mr Fox.

But I refused to be nice about it – he was a thief after all (kind of). I snatched the locket, nodded to Lex and Nicholas, and walked out of the room.

Operation Stolen Locket
SOLVED

On the way to the sitting room, I peeled off the last few bits of paper still stuck to the locket.

Carmella sat in her usual armchair.

'Hi, Carmella,' I said as Lex and Nicholas

perched on arm and the back of the chair next to her, 'look what we found.'

'My locket!' Carmella beamed and took it in her hands as if it was the most precious thing in the world. 'Did I drop it?'

'Out in the rose bush,' Nicholas said with a wink.

'In the garden? What am I like? Thanks very much for picking it up, I'd be lost without it.'

'I know you would,' I said.

'You know,' said Carmella, 'you remind me a bit of my Freddie. Do you know her? She's such a divil.'

'So I've heard.'

'Want to see a picture?'

I smiled at her and nodded. She opened the locket and showed me the photo she'd shown me a hundred times before.

'Why are we going back to Rowan Tree Manor?' asked Nicholas as we made our way from Berbel Street later that day.

I was trying not to grin, but I had a little knot of excitement in my tummy.

'Because,' I said, 'I think I might have solved Operation Catch the Cheating Cheaty Cheaters.'

'You mean Operation Weather Vane.'

'Are you talking about Operation Scavenger Hunt?' asked Lex.

I frowned. 'That title did get a bit confusing.'

'So who did it?'

'I'm not sure yet.'

'You said you solved it,' said Nicholas.

'I said I *think* I might have solved it.' We stepped on to the porch of Rowan Tree Manor and rang the bell. 'But we still have some investigating to do.'

I was expecting Graham to answer, so when Mr McCall opened the door I got a little nervous.

'Um, hello Mr McCall.'

'Yes? What is it?'

'Um, we were wondering ... I mean, I told Graham that we were, um ...'

'Yes? What?'

Mr McCall being impatient annoyed me. I decided to stand my ground.

'Mr McCall, we're investigating the disappearance of your weather vanes. Graham supports our investigation – he asked me to let him know who did it – and we'd like to check out the shed one more time. May we do that?'

Mr McCall stared at me for a minute.

'Go on then.'

I stepped off the porch, then turned back.

'Are your dogs out?'

'Yes.'

'Would you mind putting them in their kennels please?'

Mr McCall stared at me again, then huffed and stomped past us.

'Brutus, Beelzebub, Balor, *HEEL!*'

Three huge black dogs came flying around the corner and glued themselves to Mr McCall's legs as he walked towards the kennels.

'Come on,' I said. 'Let's do this quick before he decides to let them out again.'

We picked up the pace, jogging around the house and through the gardens.

'What are you looking for?' said Nicholas.

'The weather vanes.'

'But we looked for them everywhere,' said Lex. 'They're not near the shed.'

'I don't think we did look everywhere,' I replied. 'Come on.'

When we reached the shed I immediately picked my way through the crows and climbed over the fence.

'We checked the long grass already,' said Nicholas.

'We checked out there,' I said, pointing, 'cos we thought someone might have thrown the weather vane from the roof. But I don't think it was thrown.'

I pushed away the tangles of long grass and

weeds that wound themselves around the beams of the fence, right next to the wall of the shed.

'I see something!'

Lex and Nicholas hurried over the fence and helped me clear the mess.

Down in the narrow gap between the fence and the shed, half buried in weeds and mud, were two big pieces of black metal.

'That's them, that's them!' cried Lex.

It took some effort to free the weather vanes. Eventually Lex leaned on top of the fence and squeezed her arm down into the gap, while me and Nicholas stretched our arms under the fence and pushed the vanes up from below.

'Got it!' Lex pulled out one vane, then the other.

I held up a metal crow in each hand.

'We did it!'

The vanes were a bit heavy – one of them tipped over and hit me on the head. I didn't mind.

'I still don't get it though?' said Nicholas. 'Who stole them and hid them behind the fence?'

'That,' I said, 'is what our next bit of investigating will find out.'

Chapter Sixteen

I loved that we were about to run a stake-out from our very own clubhouse – it was the *perfect* stakeout location. It was hidden in a secret spot in the hedge at the end of Mr McCall's field; there were snacks in the (recently refilled) muffin tin to keep our energy up; and there were board games, crossword puzzles and other books for when any of us needed to take a break. Best of all, there was plenty of room for the three of us.

I pulled the table over to the window to stand on it, then I climbed the clubhouse wall and folded back a corner of the paddling pool roof (the paddling pool makes a great roof; it keeps out most of the rain, and if we need to climb the clubhouse tree – like we did for this mission – we can just fold it back without causing any long-term damage).

'Gimme a leg up, will you?' I said, not quite able to lift myself over the wall of the clubhouse to sit on the branch above.

Nicholas grabbed my foot and pushed me upwards.

'Cass, you still haven't told us what we're doing. Who's going to steal the weather vane?'

'I got the idea from Operation Stolen Locket,' I replied.

'That doesn't answer my question.'

I smiled down at Nicholas.

'Don't worry, you'll see them soon enough. They won't be able to help themselves … I'm pretty sure.'

Graham had arrived home before we'd left Rowan Tree Manor. He was delighted (and impressed) that we had found the two weather vanes, but I didn't want to tell him who the suspect was yet.

'I'm almost a hundred percent positive that if you replace the weather vane, it'll disappear again,' I told him. 'Will you put one of them back up?'

'I will.' Graham was smiling. 'But I'd love to know who you think the culprit is.'

'I'll tell you when I'm a hundred and ten percent sure.'

Above the clubhouse, I wriggled along the branch so Lex and Nicholas could follow me up. My binoculars hung around my neck. I peeked through them and saw that Graham was as good as his word – in the distance, a black crow-shaped weather vane sat on top of the shed in Mr McCall's garden.

'What now?' asked Lex.

'Now we watch,' I said, 'and wait.'

We waited. And waited. And waited and waited and waited and waited and waited.

Lex started fidgeting.

'Em, Cass? Nothing's happening.'

'It *will*. Give it time.'

'Okay.'

A few minutes later I got a fright when Lex suddenly tipped forward and I thought she was falling out of the tree. But she was hanging onto a branch the whole time, and she swung down so she could dangle and swing back and forth to kick at the trunk.

'Urgh, Lex! Don't do that.'

'Sorry,' she said, still dangling. 'I'm hungry.'

'Then go have a mini-muffin.'

'Do you want one?'

'No, thanks.'

''Kay.'

She did a swing-pull-up-climb thing back onto the branch, and then slid into the clubhouse like it was no effort at all. I really envied Lex sometimes.

Ten minutes later Nicholas started fidgeting.

'My legs are going numb. Mind keeping watch while I get a mini-muffin too?'

I sighed. 'Fine.'

'Think I'm gonna read for a bit as well.'

'Fine.'

'You sure you don't want a mini-muffin?'

I wanted to say no to show that I was

serious about my detective work, but my tummy was rumbling.

'Yes, please. And hand me up a crossword book, will you?'

'Sure.'

Another hour later and my whole body had gone numb. I really needed to move, but I was afraid I'd miss something.

'Cass,' Nicholas called out from the club-house, 'I'm gonna go. It's past dinner time and I'm starving.'

'Me too,' said Lex.

'Just a few more minutes,' I said, '*please*. Or you'll miss it.'

'You said that half an hour ago,' said Nicholas.

I held up the binoculars for the millionth time. The weather vane was still there.

'Okay,' I said, feeling like a deflating balloon. 'Maybe we can try again tomorrow.'

I took one last glance at the shed and saw a shadow flit across the roof.

'Wait!' I said, jamming the binoculars against my face. 'Wait! There she is!'

'Is someone stealing it?' Nicholas cried from below. 'Help me up!'

I grabbed Nicholas's arm, while Lex pushed him up from below. A minute later the three of us were bundled out onto the branch as far as we could go, passing the binoculars back and forth.

'I don't see anyone,' said Lex.

'Me neither,' said Nicholas. 'There's no one there, Cass.'

'Watch carefully,' I said.

One of the creepy black crows perched

on the roof next to the weather vane. She seemed to peck at the base of it a few times, then – just as I'd suspected – she grabbed the skinny metal bar holding the vane in place, and began to tug. The bar shunted out of one of the base's eyeholes and the weather vane tipped to one side. The crow kept tugging and the bar shunted out of the second eyehole. The weather vane smacked flat onto the slanted roof, and slid off (and, I was sure, down into the gap between the shed and the fence).

'Woah!' said Lex.

'That's so weird!' Nicholas said. 'Why did she do that?'

'I'd seen one of them do it when we were checking out the shed,' I said. 'Not stealing the bar – but I saw her use it to needle insects out of a log. Crows really are clever. I think they're my favourite animal now.'

'That's amazing, Cass! How did you even think of that?'

'The magpies. It hit me after we caught Mr Fox – I was so ready to believe that magpies were guilty of stealing the locket, but I never thought to suspect the crows of stealing the weather vane.' I tapped my temple. 'Took me a while, but I worked it out.'

Lex was grinning. 'You're a genius, Cass.'

'I know.'

'I saw it from the kitchen window!' Graham had flung open the door as soon as we arrived at Rowan Tree Manor. 'I couldn't help keeping an eye on the shed, and my goodness, who on earth would have suspected the crows? Amazing!'

'Cass did,' said Nicholas.

'You did, didn't you? I am so impressed. Listen, I have something for you guys.' Graham ducked back into the house and emerged a few seconds later with a strange golden trophy. It was in the shape of a freaky scarecrow. 'There was a mix-up with the order for this – I thought it hadn't gone through and I ordered another one and … – anyway, the point is I ended up with two of these. And I think Puzzle Pals have more than earned one.'

He handed me the scarecrow trophy. On a golden plaque on the wooden base I read the words:

Scarecrow Scavenger Hunt
WINNERS!

I smiled and tried to hide the unexpected tears that welled up in my eyes.

'Thanks, Graham.'

I held up the trophy and read the plaque one more time. I was *so* glad the team name didn't go on it.

Puzzle Pals. Ugh!

Operation Scavenger Hunt
a.k.a. Operation Catch the Cheating Cheaty Cheaters
a.k.a. Operation Weather Vane
SOLVED

I was in such a good mood on our last day working in Shady Oaks gardens, that not even Nathan could spoil it.

'What are those?' he said, pointing to a few delicate little purple buds on two of the succulent plants.

'They're eggs,' I said, without missing a beat.

'Eggs?'

'Yeah. Caterpillar eggs. Don't touch them cos, eh … I think they can be poisonous. That's how they can live on a cactus and not get sick.'

None of that made sense, but I said it with so much confidence that Nathan obviously thought it must be true.

'Oh.'

I got to my feet.

'Are you going into the centre?' he said. 'Again? Do you love it in there or something?'

'Do you know what, Nathan? I kind of do.'

I walked away with a smile on my face. Those pretty purple buds would be pretty purple flowers soon and the rock garden wouldn't be so boring after all.

Me, Lex and Nicholas had one final visit to make. We knocked on the open door of Mr Fox's room. He looked up from his book.

'You lot again? Come to take more stuff?'

'Nope,' I said. 'The opposite.'

The paper yellow rose was still looking a little sad and empty without its centre.

'What does that mean?' said Mr Fox.

I turned to Lex.

'Mr Fox,' said Lex, 'we think your art stuff is so brilliant, and we felt bad that your paper flower isn't finished anymore. So …' She reached into her pocket and held out one of her Community Games medals – a gold one she got for winning first place in the hundred-metre race. 'I think it's just about the right size.'

Mr Fox stared at the medal for a moment, then did something very unexpected – he smiled.

'It's perfect. Thank you.'

'You're very welcome.'

'Well,' Mr Fox seemed a little uncomfortable – I don't think he was used to being friendly, 'would you three like to help me with a collage?'

'Yes, please,' said Nicholas.

'Yes, please,' I repeated. 'But you don't have to smile the whole time if you don't want to.'

Mr Fox sighed in relief and gave me his usual grumbly expression. 'Thank you.'

We spent the whole rest of the afternoon making the collage. As we worked my brain was already searching for our next great adventure. Would we find out the truth about the ghost of Rowan Tree Manor? Would we discover an evil genius crow intent on taking over the world? Would we ever understand what teenagers are talking about?

This is one of the frustrating things about being a genius detective – so many mysteries, so little time.

CLUBHOUSE RULES

1.THE BUBBLE STREET GANG IS A SECRET ORGANISATION — NEVER REVEAL ITS EXISTENCE.

2. NEVER TELL ANYONE OUTSIDE THE BUBBLE STREET GANG ABOUT THE CLUBHOUSE.

3.THE BUBBLE STREET GANG SWEARS TO SEARCH OUT ADVENTURE, SOLVE MYSTERIES, FIGHT FOR JUSTICE AND BE GOOD ~~ENTERPRINEERS~~ ~~ENTREPENORS~~ BUSINESSPEOPLE.

4.NO FRUIT, BROWN BREAD OR OTHER HEALTHY FOOD IS TO BE CONSUMED IN THE CLUBHOUSE.

5.THE CLUBHOUSE LIBRARY IS FOR EXCITING, DANGEROUS, DETECTIVE OR FUNNY BOOKS ONLY. NO SCHOOLBOOKS.

6.MEMBERS WILL TAKE TURNS TO REFILL THE SNACK JARS.

7.ALWAYS CLOSE THE CLUBHOUSE DOOR WHEN YOU ARE LAST OUT.

8.SECRET DOCUMENTS MUST BE LOCKED AWAY IN THE HARRY POTTER BOOK–SAFE DURING THE NIGHT.

9.IF YOU'RE EATING SOMETHING CRUMBLY YOU MUST USE A PLATE. NO–ONE WANTS MICE IN THE CLUBHOUSE.

10.ANY MEMBER CAN DEMAND HELP FROM OTHER MEMBERS IN MATTERS OF LIFE OR DEATH (OR IF IT'S JUST REALLY, REALLY IMPORTANT).

ANYONE WHO BREAKS ANY OF THE RULES OF THE CLUBHOUSE
MUST BE PUNISHED.

Ringland
4/9/20
Library